It Happened That Night

A tale of love, deceit and murder

It Happened That Night

A tale of love, deceit and murder

Akash Verma

Srishti
PUBLISHERS & DISTRIBUTORS

Srishti Publishers & Distributors
N-16, C. R. Park
New Delhi 110 019
editorial@srishtipublishers.com

First published by
Srishti Publishers & Distributors in 2010

10 9

Printed and bound in India

For my Mother and Ura

Acknowledgement

I am so glad that you are finally reading my story. You would have shelled out a hundred bucks to buy this book and I sincerely hope that this exceeds your expectations.

The eighteen month long process in writing my first book has truly been exhilarating and a journey of self discovery. I suddenly feel that I have a lot to say. Really! It was difficult to start initially and I had to push myself into putting my fingers on to the lap top but once I started typing, there was no looking back. Airplane, train, car, in between weddings, early mornings, afternoons , late nights, hotels… name the place or the time and this book would have been written there and then. The urge to reach you and tell you a story was so strong that it crossed all hurdles.

I actually feel a bit sad having finished this book and with this particular last piece of acknowledgement going away from the lives of Chandan and Bhavna. Nevertheless you getting to know them and reading their story is a new high for me which is heart-warming. When I narrated the outline of this book to some of my friends, they saw an uncanny similarity between my past work life and the setting of this novel and presumed whether the book was autobiographical. Even my publisher commented that. My answer to their query is an emphatic "No". This is a complete work of fiction and has no bearing with any real life instances. Obviously like any creative mind would, you do borrow references from people, incidents and some real happenings. But this is no true story or anything close to that for sure.

I am grateful to everyone around me who made this happen and will keep making this happen again and again. The team from Srishti publishers for being absolutely wonderful right from the start and boosting my confidence that my story had everything in it to be heard. Lastly to you who are holding this book in your hand ready to embark on a hopefully memorable journey. I cherish your contribution the most.

Let's catch up again. Soon!

1
Amdavad

I turned on the ignition of my white Maruti 800 and put it in reverse gear while adjusting my rear view mirror. The car parked next to mine was a big fat Honda City and had no intention of giving me any space to move out.

'These assholes! Why do they buy big cars when they don't know how to park them?' I cursed as I backed my car in Navyug Apartments, Vastrapur, Ahmedabad.

It was February morning and the breeze felt cool despite the clock hitting 9. I rolled down the driver window a bit for ventilation and pressed the cassette into the recorder. By the time my car left the main gate of the apartment, Jim Morrison had started belting out Light My Fire.

I had moved into Ahmedabad from Pune a fortnight back and was a bit disappointed to be here. Pune with its lovely weather, friendly people and entertainment options (read bars and swanky pubs) was a rocking city. It had this unique quality of being a cosmopolitan place that held on to its small town roots. It did not intimidate people like me who were born and brought up in small towns but welcomed them and made them a part of its own set up. Ahmedabad was a bit confusing. While there was money and prosperity all around, the city lacked inclusiveness. The local society was open, friendly and ready to talk to you, but would never absorb you. I summed up the essence of my *Amdavad* understanding while talking to my dad the other day. 'You can stay but not live in Ahmedabad.'

I work here as a Marketing Manager for The Uni-Cola Company, the largest beverage brand in the world with a footprint in 200 countries across the globe. It is among the top 10 most valuable brands in the world. A mere mention of the company name in a social gathering is enough to evoke magical responses like Oh, Wow, Great etc. Frankly, I have always enjoyed this attention from the opposite sex, besides a never ending admiration from the PPOUW society (*Psyched Parents of Unmarried Women*). I have been with Uni-Cola for last 4 years through which they made me run across Mumbai, Pune before landing me into Ahmedabad. I used to work with an advertising agency that serviced The Uni- Cola Company where I was their client servicing manager. I managed to impress the Marketing Head of TUCC (always *read as The Uni-Cola Company from now*) to such an extent that he offered me a position within the company and I gladly stuck to the offer like a leech.

Some more dope on me to build familiarity. I am the only son in a middle class family that has its roots in Uttar Pradesh. My father has been in the finance department of a public sector fertilizer organization for all 30-35 years of his working life. The job has paid him enough to have a two bedroom house in Lucknow and his monthly pension takes care of the house that he and my mother occupy. My mother, also from the same Kayastha community as my father, has been an able and doting home-maker (*modern day terminology for a housewife who does not do anything except house work, commercially non productive to be precise*). A major part of my childhood has been spent in Kanpur where I studied in a convent school while my college happened in the Lucknow University. After spending an unforgettable time in the heartland I moved to Delhi where I did my MBA before joining the advertising world. While I may consider my home to be Delhi, because that's the common career capital for all white collared North Indians , my roots are still in UP. I had left UP after my college and have been on my own for last 6-7 years. Quite eventful, free and spaced out seven years. My story unfolds after that in February 2002.

'You speak English but you think in Hindi, truly a Bhaiyya,' laughed Bhavna.

'Oh really! And where are you from? United States? Brought up in Mumbai but born and educated at Nasik a part of rural Maharashtra and then you think yourself to be an uptown girl?' I snapped back.

2
The Cola Land

It took me about five minutes to reach the TUCC local sales office in Thaltej. As my Maruti rolled, Shahnawaz Khan the Bollywood superstar greeted me with a bottle of Unicola in his hand, perched atop the back of a Tata 407, also called a *route vehicle* in the soft drink industry lingo. Entering the TUCC sales depot in the morning makes you feel as if you are entering a battle field with army tanks all around, big and intimidating.

As I got of the car, I saw Atul Parikh the Area Sales Manager and Ratnesh Pathak his sales executive, conducting the morning meeting with the entire distributor salesman team. Looking disinterested but standing with them was Dakshesh Bhai the 26 year old fat son of Kalpesh Bhai, the TUCC distributor for New Ahmedabad. Morning meeting in the soft drink industry is an every-day ritual, comparable to the morning prayers of an average Hindu. You just can't start your day without it. The sales executives hold it every morning before the trucks leave for selling soft-drinks in the market. These meetings are akin to the pre-war ritual of the ancient times where the army was armed and prepared appropriately to face the enemy before the battle. The battlegrounds may have changed but the tactics remained the same. In our case the enemy was TACC a.k.a. The American Cola Company. I am quite certain that every morning the Area Sales Manager or the sales executive who is conducting the morning meeting feels empowered like the CEO of an organization or an army general marshalling his troupes would, and gets a hard-on. What he doesn't realize is that more than half of his troupe comprising of salesman actually care a fuck. These are the guys who have been in this hardcore soft drink business upwards of fifteen years, plying their tanks (read trucks) on the same routes, going to the same shops, selling the same black stuff and doing the same things each day. Deep down, they are quite sure that management studs like us in the company will come, give some *gyaan* and go away but they will stay where they are, doing the same things today that they were doing ten years earlier. Somehow they know that they are the real studs who run companies like TUCC.

Global soft-drink giants like TUCC re-entered the Indian market in the early nineties after being unceremoniously kicked out of the country during the emergency in the seventies. In the last 17-18 years of the re-emergence of the soft drink industry in India, it has been dominated by two global players TUCC and TACC (The American Cola Comapnay). TUCC was the older global brand that captured the consumer's fancy and faith in the late nineteenth century and by the seventies became the world's top brand. While TACC was a late entrant into the market, with its youthful positioning and strong marketing, it was giving TUCC a run for its money in many European and Asian Markets. India with its never dwindling promise of a billion people is the land of opportunity for any and every business across the globe. I have yet to see a business presentation on India that does not begin with "India – The land of Opportunities" as the first slide. I am sure both TUCC and TACC saw and evaluated a similar presentation in the early nineties and jumped into the land, hoping to strike rich early, and make the Wall Street and their share holder's dance to their tunes. Perhaps what they could not comprehend at that time was that despite there being millions of parched throats in the country, there were an equal number of empty pockets. While there was a substantial middle class population in India, fifty percent of India still lived in villages. And while the country had an intimidating young population, equally alarming was its unemployment. Both the companies invested heavily in infrastructure, marketing along with people and even after 15-16 years of operations, could not break even. For how long could the big daddies sitting in America feed their poor Indian babies? Pressure was building up on the Indian operations of the soft-drink companies to deliver both top-line and bottom-line i.e.sales and profit. This made competition fierce and slimy; both the players fought very hard each day and were ready to use any tactic to grab that elusive market share.

I smiled at the guys and greeted Dakshesh with '*Kem Chho Dakshesh Bhai*?' in local Gujarati. '*Saaru Chandan Bhai, Tame kem chho*?' Dakshesh replied with a dumb and unwilling smile as if someone was holding on to his fat lips. My sales executives respectfully wished me and paved way for me to pass. I climbed the flight of stairs quickly, looking at the bunch of kids playing cricket on the ground next to the sales office. The Thaltej Sales office of TUCC was an office cum depot that was taken on rent by Dakshsesh the company distributor. The company obviously paid for all the costs incurred by the distributor and offered him a decent return on investment of 20% + , but still he was perpetually unhappy. Maria, the administration assistant at the sales office greeted me with a wide smile as I entered my cabin. I plugged in my laptop and by the time Lotus Notes opened I had made a quick visit to the loo and ordered tea from the pantry on my way back. I checked my e-mail in half an hour and looked at my watch. It was 10.15.

'Where the hell is DK? Bugger is never on time?' I muttered to myself and picked up the phone to check with Maria, who told me that he had not arrived as yet. DK Sanyal was my Assistant Marketing Manger and had worked his way up the ladder from being a sales executive in a soap company in the eighties. He would be pushing forty but looked close to forty five. TUCC during its launch phase in early nineties wanted a big bang launch in Gujarat which was one of their critical Indian markets. DK Sanyal had apparently done a very good job in launching a new soap variant at that time in his earlier company and that new soap was plastered across the state on hoardings, wall paintings and other forms of local media. The story goes that one of the American General Manager of TUCC, who was the in-charge of setting up operations in Gujarat, got so impressed after seeing the soap visibility, that he asked the local team to hire DK immediately at double his salary. 'This guy will paint the town red for us,' he said. Red was the brand color of TUCC. DK was a master of the advertising and publicity material business. He could tell you the standard per square feet cost of a glow-sign and also tell you who could give you that at the cheapest rates in Gujarat. He could also tell you the difference between the quality of two posters stuck on the wall along with their costs and also who their possible printers were. It worked well for DK initially but soon this *USP (Unique Selling Proposition)* of his waned as other functional pluses such as brand understanding, strategic thinking, research and planning gained more prominence within the TUCC marketing function. DK never graduated or tried to imbibe these new functional competencies. I would personify him as Brijesh Khanna the superstar of yester years, who still thought that dancing around trees with an un-tucked shirt and flicking his hands as if one were distributing currency, would have the same effect on the movie-goer now. It could not work simply because India had moved to dirty dancing in an air-conditioned disco. DK was caught in a time warp and he simply did not want to get out of it. He would often say that strategy, vision and thought had no role to play in building a brand and that a brand could only stay alive till the time it was on a hoarding, poster or a wall-painting on a shop. To him Jack Welch would be some Hollywood Star of sixties. DK also carried a sense of arrogance with him that came to him because of his age and 20 years of work experience. I was pretty sure that during our interaction over the last few days he thought about me as some new kid on the block who was his boss because of studying in some fancy business school and knowing some marketing jargons which made no sense in the real world. I hated this.

At 10.45 DK peeped into the room, 'Were you looking for me?' he said with a straight face.

Not wanting to look up and with my eyes on the laptop, I said, 'Where were you dude? Why are you so late for work when there is a consumer promotion campaign on?'

'Did the second earthquake take place in an hour, what's the big deal?' he snapped back. Perhaps being called a dude irritated him.

Gujarat in 2001 had witnessed a disastrous earthquake and its effect did not seem to leave the lives of the people staying here. I felt like retorting but somehow restrained my-self.

'What is Dakshesh Bhai saying about the promotion? Is it working and impacting sales? Are we able to get entry into new shops through this? What is the consumer saying? What about competition?' My flurry of questions stumped DK and he seemed out of place.

'Umm.., well it looks a bit early ...Uh I checked with Dakshesh but as always he is not very co-operative. I need to check the data on new outlets for the last three days,' he said. Like Alexander the great who did not want to screw an already vanquished Porus, I replied, 'That is fine DK, let us go down to Dakshesh and find out right now.'

In modern day business, initiative and proactiveness are two key skills that a manager should have. I wanted to demonstrate that to my co-worker and create one more dent on his self inflated ego. DK followed me like a Labrador who had just been spanked by his master. I quickly went down the stairs and walked with a swagger to Dakshesh's room.

'Chandan, you walk like a wrestler…why can't you walk normally?' Bhavna said.

'Arrey I do that more when I am feeling good,' I said.

'So pretentious you are, you bloody Bhaiyyaji,' she chuckled from behind.

3
Us and Them

TUCC's city office at Thaltej was a distributor godown on the ground floor with a small sales office on the first. There were three rooms on the ground floor. The entrance led to the bigger room where a couple of Dakshesh's accountants sat and the rest of the space was utilized by the 20 odd route salesmen in the mornings and late evenings after a hard days work. On the right hand side of the entrance was the cashier Anwar's table, the most crowded place after 7 pm, where all the agents returned to settle the accounts before they retired. On the left was Dakshesh's room where he sat along with his father. TUCC distributorship was one of his businesses; the other's included a couple of petrol pumps in old Ahmedabad and distributorship of the No.2 mobile handset company in India. He would give about 4-5 hours of his working time on an average to the soft-drink business each day.

Dakshesh was sitting in his den and playing PACMAN when we entered his air-conditioned room. He glanced as us and gave us an indifferent smile. His father, Kalpesh Bhai did not even attempt that and was glued to his files as if he was looking at a map that lead him to the treasure of Alibaba.

'So Dakshesh Bhai how have the sales been for the last 3 days? How is the promotion doing?' I said.

I was curious to know the promotion impact as we were doing an under the crown consumer promotion in India after a long time.

TUCC was promoting it heavily across all media including cable and satellite television. The consumer could stand to win from Rs.10 to a crore of rupees under the Uni-Cola bottle cap and the probability of winning was one in five, which was fairly good.

'What sir! Not enough company support, no scheme on the stocks and the ad that I saw on TV last night, was also not that catchy. Did you see the new TACC ad, sir? What an ad! Really good; our marketing people at Delhi are not doing much. TACC marketing is much better,' he said.

He had paused the game while muttering this crap and was by now looking into my eyes as if I was an idiot who had just come out of the Agra Mental Asylum.

I tried to hold on to my sudden rush of blood, 'Dakshesh how many new outlets have we gone to? Is the sales up because of the promotion? Has there been any impact?' The tone of my voice made it clear that I did not like his shitty reply, and was in no mood to support his sob story of an additional market discount scheme along with millions of rupees of consumer promotion.

'Chandan Bhai, no major difference, sales is up by about 10 % but from the same outlets. Outlet coverage is also similar on almost every route, though we are trying,' he said trying to cover up his laziness under the garb of promotion not being effective enough.

I was not in a mood to take shit. 'That is the whole issue with you guys? TUCC is doing an Under the Crown promotion for the first time in 3 years and there is hardly any impact in the area of biggest distributor of Ahmedabad controlling 60% of the market. I would want to know how many new outlets we went on each route over the last three days and how many of them said no to TUCC stocks,' I said.

Dakshesh fumbled and tried to murmur something but before he could open his mouth, I had turned towards DK, 'So how many outlets have we been able to merchandise (putting advertising material like posters etc. on shops) over last three days, what is the percentage DK?' DK was as clueless as he was ten minutes back.

Kalpesh Bhai who was till now an ear witness to our conversation was in no mood to see his son losing the battle to a 28 year old TUCC Marketing Manager. He suddenly threw a beamer at me.

'The company expects the distributor to do all this, but what about our commission? It has been the same for last three years; do you think our expenses have not gone up? What is the company doing about it?' he said.

This was a scud missile out of nowhere and tough to intercept because distributors in western India had formed an association that had been raising this issue for quite some time. They had been pressurizing the soft-drink lobby to raise the commission and that had resulted into state wide protests, even stalling production at some soft-drink plants. Seeing his father resurrecting him at this juncture, Dakshesh who was quite like a knocked out boxer, also tried to jump back into the ring in an attempt to redeem his glory. 'Yes, yes Chandan Bhai, all these questions are fine but what about our commission?'

'Look guys; let us not mix up the two issues....,' I was stopped in the middle of my sentence as Anwar Bhai the fifty five year old cashier barged inside the room with two route agents Hiren and Jignesh.

'What brings you here now? And why haven't you left for your routes,' Kalpesh asked in an irritated voice.

Both the route agents looked visibly angry with Anwar and looked at him with disdain. Anwar answered in a complaining manner, 'Kalpesh sir, I just cannot take this. These guys have given a credit of forty five thousand rupees in the market and even after repeated follow ups with them for over fifteen days now; they have not got anything back. Till the time they pay back, I am not going to allow them to do business in the market. They cannot leave this godown with their trucks.'

Hiren hissed at him like a snake, 'So what? Anwar you bloody plant your dirty ass in the office and keep giving orders to us? Do you know how many cases we sell everyday? Your salary comes because of the hard-work that we do, so do not order us. Let me see how can you stop us? So what if we have given away some credit in the market? It is only to get sales for the company, and we will get it back ourselves. But we are not here to take your orders, gotcha. Kalpesh Bhai please tell this kid not to throw his weight around.'

I was amazed at the outburst of the route agents and their cheek to talk like this in front of us. Hiren and Jignesh were the oldest and supposedly best route agents that Dakshesh had. They operated on the "golden routes" of Ahmedabad; Satellite and Ashram Road. Daily average sale of Hiren and Jignesh was more than double than that of the other routes in Ahmedabad. But more than that, they were old confidantes of Kalpesh Bhai. Both of them were nearing fifty and had been associated with Kalpesh Bhai for the last thirty years. It was rumored that they were privy to a lot of business and private secrets of Kalpesh's family. Right from the underhand dealings that Kalpesh Bhai did while setting up his big business to the clandestine affairs. On top of this they had taken good care of Dakshesh while he was growing up and were like his mentor when he took over the distributorship of TUCC.

I knew the odds were against Anwar.

Kalpesh Bhai announced like an emperor, 'Anwar Bhai, let them go and in future never talk to them like this. After all they are our best people. Give their records to me and in future if there are any issues, inform me first.'

Anwar's face fell; I guess he was unhappy with the fact that Kalpesh failed to acknowledge his honesty to the job and surrendered to the baseless talk of the uncouth agents. I wanted to demonstrate my displeasure with this incident but this was getting into the distributor turf. I restrained myself. This small incident of complete favoritism had taken me away from Shahnawaz Khan and his Under the Crown promotion. I left the room and heard Dakshesh speaking in the background, 'Puppa it is always better to employ only Hindus in the company, otherwise there will always be confrontations like this.'

Hinduism was taking its precedence in the country in these times and phrases like "India only for Hindus" were the latest buzzword. The Indian diaspora had suddenly realized that they could get a sense of belonging by uniting under the Hindu umbrella. The new "Hindu" identity was on the upswing and this was reflected in the changing political dynamics in the country with parties floating the Hindu Charter suddenly gaining popularity and voter support. While walking out of Dakshesh's room I felt weak in my knees for not speaking up at a time when bias was flying all around me.

'What can I do, it's their business?' I consoled myself and entered my cabin.

When I came out of the wash room, Bhavna was humming, 'Honesty is such a lonely word. Every body is so untrue.'

'Is this your favorite song?' I asked her.

'You know what? I love the lyrics. An honest person is always alone.'

I shrugged as if it was difficult to understand.

4
Sumo – The Tiger

Sumo, my boss called. We fixed up a time of 2pm to meet at his office in the TUCC plant near Nadiad on the Vadodara Highway.

Sumanto Sen a.k.a Sumo was in his late thirties and was one of the youngest General Managers of TUCC company. He came from a lower middle class Bengali family in Calcutta, and was the only son of his parents after three daughters in a row. Sumo's education was dependant on scholarships and soon he realized that struggle was imperative to his life. After graduating from Calcutta he went on to do his masters from the rural management institute at Anand in Gujarat. Sumo at one time was a socialist who believed in an ideal state that provided equal opportunities and uniform distribution of wealth. But his struggles in the real world taught him pretty fast that opportunities do not just come by, one needs to grab them by the throat. You need to fight it out, he used to say. Sumo started his career with a co-operative dairy organization in Gujarat, but soon got disillusioned with the rapid success that his peers from management school were achieving in other multi-national companies. It is rumored that he got really lucky one day. While watching an India-Sri-Lanka One Day Cricket Match at Eden Gardens in mid nineties, he caught the eyes of Don Brown the President of TUCC for South East Asia, who sat there during one of his market visits to the East India. Sumo was in the first row, loudly cheering for the Indian team holding the tri-coloured Indian flag in one hand

and a bottle of Uni-Cola in the other one. Whenever a Sri Lankan batsman got out he would break into an impromptu jig and spray the cola on the crowd around, as if he had a champagne bottle in his hand.

Don was very impressed watching the antiques of this five feet two inches Indian and he remarked, 'If this bloke can show so much of passion on the cricket field, he would be a tiger in the market. This guy will draw blood.'

Sumo was called next day to the TUCC office in Delhi and offered the job of a Sales Manger in Patna. the rustic capital of Bihar. Sumo turned Bihar upside down with his hard work, inhibited aggression and understanding of Indian ground realities. His super performance there earned him the tag of "Tiger" in the TUCC system. Over the last six years within TUCC, Sumo had mellowed down, but the sparks still remained coupled with patches of raw aggression.

I looked at my watch, it was 12.45 pm. The plant was about 40 kilometers away from the city office and it was time for me to get going. After off-loading some of my "Things to Do" for the day to DK, I embarked on my long drive to the plant. I looked at my watch again at Vishala, the much famous authentic Gujarati restaurant at Vasna. A few luxury coaches were parked neatly outside Vishala, and reminded me of the TUCC Tata 407's parked in disarray within Dakshesh's go-down. My thought wandered back to the morning incident and finally got seized on to the repulsive faces of Hiren and Jignesh. They still had the same smirk on their ugly lips. I took a right turn from the Naroda circle towards Vadodara. Small eateries and restaurant flocked the highway on both sides, with TUCC and TACC glow-signs hanging at their top, in a bid to woo the thirsty consumer 'Our visibility is getting less here; TACC is going aggressive purposely because these outlets are en-route to our plant. They are doing this deliberately and DK does not even know it. Why isn't he proactive enough on all these things? When will DK get a handle on these things which are strategically important?' I wished my thoughts could be conveyed as they were, at the same moment, to DK but I was no Captain Kirk of Starship Enterprise.

I reached the TUCC plant at 1.45 pm and entered Sumo's cabin. He was engrossed in his lap top with his back towards me.

'Hi Chandan how are you?' he said.

'I am good Sumo, how have you been and how did you know it was me?' I exclaimed. Sumo laughed, and got up. He walked towards me and put his hand around my shoulders, 'Let's have lunch.'

The TUCC pantry was on the ground floor and could accommodate about two hundred people. Everyone ate there, right from a worker on the manufacturing line to Sumo. The two of us took a few chapattis, dal and some vegetable along with a bottle of Uni-Cola. We sat near the window seat overlooking the godown. The godown looked completely choc a bloc with stocks of Uni-Cola.

'The product does not seem to be moving these days though this it's not even winter time here,' I thought, and intuitively looked towards Sumo knowing well that the story in his mind would be similar.

Sumo started off, 'The promotion does not seem to be doing very well in the first week Chandan. In spite of heavy advertising, I do not think we would be doing 20% incremental sales in this quarter as compared to last year. This is what I have promised my boss for this quarter. I think we need to do something more, push sales in the market through some lucrative scheme. There is still some time.'

'But Sumo the promotion has just started and it is very early to base a hypothesis on. I agree with you that it has not pushed up sales from the word go, but I am sure that as awareness builds up through television and local advertising, we will surely see some consumer traction. I do not see why we should be giving away another market scheme or doing a sales incentive despite a million dollar consumer promotion?' I said.

Sumo continued as if he had not heard me, 'Chandan, you are new to this market, and consumer promotions like Under the Crown do not turn the market upside down. Max it will do is build a bit of consumer demand. But that's not enough and you just can't bet your life on it. And for us here, quarterly sales targets are our life,' Sumo said looking a bit irritated as if reprimanding his five year old son.

'But Sumo it is not summer as yet, you can't create an artificial demand in the market, let's give it some more time please,' I said.

He had turned philosophical by now, looked askance towards the window and pointed towards the thousands of cases of Uni-Cola placed on top of each other, 'You see those filled cases Chandan? Either we do something extra to sell them, or live with the current situation. If that be the case, why does the Uni-Cola management need competent people like you and me? They would let only salesmen run the business.'

Impressed with his Steve Jobs speech he expected a standing ovation from me.

I knew wasting any more time on this would be futile, 'Okay what is on your mind Sumo? What should we do?'

Sumo's eyes gleamed wickedly and I knew something was coming, 'What do you think appeals to a sales guy Chandan?'

'Well cash, holiday, gifts such as durables,' I blurted out these things as they were SOPs (Standard Operating Principles) of incentives within the FMCG industry.

'Well what about women?' he said.

'What about that, a woman appeals to every man on this planet, forget only sales people?' I wondered where this conversation was leading to.

'I was in Mumbai last week and had gone to a dance bar. I saw people almost ready to give their lives to those good looking bar dancers. Why can't we get those dancers in Ahmedabad to put up a similar performance? In lieu of this motivational exercise we can also take commitments from the sales teams on delivering sales targets that very night. I am sure once these dancers charm them to agree on these sales targets we can hold them accountable as well,' Sumo exploded all keyed up.

'What are you saying Sumo?' I just couldn't help being loud.

Sumo looked at me as if I had refused a date with Angelina Jolie.

'Let's do it man, it will be unique and very motivating for the sales force. On top of that we will get them to commit to these targets. I am telling you it will work,' Sumo said excited like a schoolboy.

'But from where do we get these sleazy dancers and where will we do this? Gujarat is a dry state and this kind of a bash is illegal. What if we invite police trouble and get bad media on this one?' I tried to put the fear of consequences and media into Sumo's head, but by now he had made up his mind.

'*Tu Dekh le yaar* (You take care of it my friend). Marketing can arrange for all this and we will do it discreetly in a resort away from the city, at one of our key accounts. No one will get to know about it. Higher the risk, bigger is the success,' Sumo said and ended the conversation.

'Let us freeze it for the Saturday, week after next, so you have two weeks to get this done,' he said.

The Marketing Manager of TUCC, representing one of the most respected companies in the world would now have to don the role of a pimp and get some third class women to dance in front of a drunken crowd.

'This is where all your strategy, insight and big picture will go Mr. Mathur, in hunting down bar dancers in Gujarat,' I thought feeling frustrated and angry as I drove out of the TUCC plant.

'Why do you have to agree with your boss all the time, when you know that he is wrong?' she asked.

'Because I give him the benefit of doubt. Ha! You just can't keep fighting with your boss forever. To reach a consensus you need to give in a few times as well,' I tried to push reason into the talk.

'But is it fair that you end up losing most of the times? That is a screwed up philosophy,' she said coldly.

5
Knocked Out

My mobile phone rang at 7.30am on Wednesday and woke me up. Atul from the advertising agency sounded very excited for having fixed four meetings with representatives from newspapers and television channels for pushing PR on TUCC Under the crown consumer promotion.

A couple of days had passed post my meeting with Sumo and I had made decent progress on both the tasks assigned to me. I was meeting four media companies today to push the consumer promotion while the other Herculean task of getting the dancers was delegated to Basant Bhatt my other Assistant Marketing Manager a.k.a B2. I reached office at 9.30 and passed the morning parade i.e. morning meeting, being orchestrated by sales executives and Dakshesh, who looked as if he was still half asleep. Monday's incident had left me disgusted and I was in no mood to have any kind of conversation with the father and son duo for some time. I gave him a wry smile and climbed up the stairs to the sales office. B2 was completely engrossed in his PC and it pleased my ego to see him early in the morning and working, unlike his other counterpart DK, who would usually walk in at 10.30 am.

'So B2 what's up? Working hard so early on something?'

B2 turned back and looked at me with his drowsy and drunk eyes, 'What to do Boss? This Prashant Bhai from City One Multiplex called me up at 9 PM last night and asked me to come up with a good proposal for exclusivity in his multiplex. He has also called TACC marketing guys for the pitch and he is going to decide by tomorrow, who is he going with. I am just drafting his proposal, will then show it to you before I meet him.' 'Yeah sure!' I said while entering my cabin.

My first meeting was at 10.30 with Gujarat Prakash, one of the most popular Gujarati dailies in the state. The team from the publication met me and I sold them the entire consumer advantage angle of under the crown promotion and how much could the consumer benefit if they consumed a Uni-Cola bottle. They promised to cover the promotion editorially in their newspaper in the coming week. More than my spiel, perhaps a commitment of two half page advertisements in their publication worked stronger.

Maria called at noon on my extension and told me that a lady from News Plus was waiting for me at the reception. News-plus was one of the largest television networks in the country with eight different channels in spaces such as general entertainment, news, sports, music, Bollywood movies etc. It had regional offices across all key states in the country and the network had a lot of credibility and eye-balls in India.

'Good, must be their local correspondent,' I thought as I asked Maria to send her in.

'Hi Chandan, I am Bhavna!' a beaming smile greeted me as she entered my room. It was the most beautiful smile that I had seen in my entire life, a smile that stretched from one ear on her face to the other. It reminded me of the "smiling face" sketch that every kid draws on his or her white drawing sheet in school. It took me a few seconds to gather myself before, I could focus on her.

'So how is it going for you guys in Gujarat? The season would be lean a bit as summers are due to start in a while? So how are you guys preparing for the season, starting with your Under the Crown consumer promotion? Yeah! Atul told me about it,' chuckled Bhavna.

'Well since you know the answer, why are you asking me?' I said in an irritated tone. 'Because I may get something more out of the Uni-Cola Marketing Head that his poor agency guy may not know,' she said and laughed.

There was something very intriguing about her. She was not conventionally beautiful but still attractiveness personified in a five feet three inch plus frame. Indian guys within the marriageable age bracket of 26 to 30 years are usually very confused. Either they lust for every second girl they see, or they look at every girl as their prospective soul-mate. I decided to steer my thoughts away from the lady sitting in front of me, to a more professional discussion about how Under the Crown consumer promotion is a unique way to reward consumers who drank Uni-Cola. After finishing my ten minute spiel, I was sure that the lady would be convinced.

'What will you have, some tea, coffee or Uni-Cola?' I said.

'What's new about your promotion? It is like serving some Indian whisky in a Chivas Regal Bottle. How many people are going to get the top prize of 1 crore? I am sure the probability of winning big prizes is not one in three and most of the consumers would get "Try Again" or "Rs.10" under the crown. Do you guys think that a Shahnawaz Khan will be able to seduce a Gujarati consumer and your sales will double? You guys really under-estimate the consumer,' she said hurriedly.

'She and Sumo would surely be related somehow. Both of them do not believe in this sexy marketing campaign. And what cheek she has comparing this big promotion to a local Indian whiskey?' I thought to myself and could feel my fondness towards her vanishing like a bubble.

'Oh, does a gentleman called Anwar Bhai work with you guys?' she said out of no where as I was getting ready for a bout of confrontation with her.

'Now, where does Anwar Bhai come in? Yes he works for us, here with my distributor downstairs. How do you know him?' I said annoyingly as if some one had ordered Pao Bhaji in an up market Italian restaurant.

Bhavna was visibly excited, 'Great, can I please meet him? Will you call for him? Actually he used to work with my father and handled finances for one of his units in Mumbai. Unfortunately he has an ailing wife and a family in Ahmedabad. A couple of years back her condition worsened and he had to come back here. Well I am very fond of him, as he was like our family member for twelve years. I have been in Ahmedabad for last six months and desperately wanted to meet him earlier. I knew he was with Uni-Cola but did not know where. So thank you Mr. Mathur, at least one good thing that your promotion could do to me. It made me come here and find out where Anwar Bhai was. Can I meet him now please?'

Amazed at her first meeting cockiness, I called for Anwar Bhai. I continued my hard sell to a media journalist mean-while, 'Well Bhavna this promotion is not all that frivolous and old, the mechanism is quite unique and interesting, it's actually for the first time that Uni-Cola is doing it in India.......'

'Hello Anwar Bhai, so good to see you!' Bhavna cut me off and jumped off the chair to hug him and then touched his feet.

I was charmed to see this exchange of pure Indian emotions in the business office of a multi-national company. She held his hand and made him sit on the chair next to her as naturally as if she was offering him a seat in her personal living room. Poor Anwar Bhai did not know what to do, but he hesitatingly sat down with his gaze oscillating between our faces. It was apparent that he was very happy to see her, but a bit perplexed as well to meet her at the Uni-Cola office of all places, and that too with me a virtual non helpful stranger. Bhavna made him comfortable by bombarding him with a lot of personal questions that ranged from the condition of his ailing wife to his young sons, from his house to his current job. I sat in front of them with my eyes transfixed on the ongoing cinema of emotions playing in front of me.

An office boy from downstairs knocked on the door and told Anwar Bhai to come to the office as Dakshesh was calling him. Anwar Bhai gathered his slender frame and stood up. His eyes were a bit moist, 'Thank you baby for seeing me, reminded me of the old times at Mumbai. We would wait for you to visit us at home. I will personally cook your favorite mutton biryani that day. Thank you Sir,' he said and walked towards the door. Bhavna "baby" got up and stepped out of my cabin to see him off. I was wondering which baby on this earth would be so aggressive, cocky and yet emotional.

Bhavna came back inside beaming and did not sit down, 'Hey thanks Chandan, you made my day by getting me to meet Anwar Bhai. In return, I will not give you any more trouble about your promotion, but will try and accommodate it in the business segment, if not the main story,' she said.

'Now don't feel bad, even the business segment gets rotated once every two hours on our channel so you will get a fair amount of publicity. I will do the story by capturing some shots of the go-down along with some outlet and publicity material pictures. I would also like to put you on TV, not sitting here in the office but outside in a real outlet. That should look much natural and better. Do you have any good outlets around Ashram Road where we could do this tomorrow?" she said.

That sounded good, I thought to myself, quite happy with her concept and the story she intended to do.

'Sounds good! Yeah we do have Shivam Stores near Ashram road which should be a good location. What time do we meet there tomorrow?' I said.

'Why don't you pick me up from the office? My television crew can follow us. Right?' she said.

She did not bother to wait for my affirmation and opened my cabin door to leave but turned around at the last moment, 'Please don't be late as I have another meeting at 7 back in my office. And just because we are covering your promotion it does not become Chivas, it still remains a local Indian whiskey,' she giggled and disappeared.

I realized after she had left, that I was happier with the prospect of meeting Bhavna the following day than getting a good story done on Uni-Cola's Under the Crown promotion.

6
Butterflies In The Stomach

I left Thaltej sales office at 3.30pm for the News Plus interview. More than twenty four hours had passed since Bhavna vanished from my office, and I would have thought of her for at-least twenty four hundred times. A mixed feeling of anxiety and delight gripped me from the time I woke up in the morning. It was supposed to be a business interview and I was behaving as if going on my first date. 'Why Chandan?' I asked myself this question repeatedly and unsuccessfully.

'You are going to meet an attractive and smart television journalist. Interview over, deal over. She goes her way and you go yours, so why this anxiousness? You come back and get going on that dancers gig with sales team. That is your circle of life dude and there is hardly any time left.' Some respite from Bhavna this thought gave me, as I reached Ashram road after taking a left from Mithakali ChaarRasta.

I parked my car on the main road in front of Bhavna's office at Akashdeep building and called her on the mobile.

'Hey, Chandan you have reached? Bang on time. Will be down in a couple of minutes,' she chirped, and hung up.

I had taken Bhavna's number from Atul, but wondered where had she got my number from? Nevertheless it was a happy feeling to have that she actually had my number stored on her handset. Her two minutes seemed like twenty but eventually I saw her walking down in a pair of jeans and a pink Tee that had 'Peace' symbol on it.

I admired her striking beauty from a distance as I saw her coming closer. With an attractive skin, an out of the world smile, shoulder length hair and a right sized body, Bhavna was very attractive by all means.

'Were you leching at me by any chance Mr. Mathur?' she giggled as she got into my Maruti and sat next to me.

I was at a loss of words after being caught in the act and nothing except a feeble smile showed up on my face.

'Not at all, I was lost in my thought that is it. Why don't you keep your bag on the back seat and be comfortable. Should we get going?' I said.

'Just hang on for a while; my crew would be coming down in a minute. They will follow us,' she said while scrutinizing the entrance.

Silence fell between us, and I squirmed on my seat, feeling her so close to me.

'Here they are! We should move and they will follow us,' she said and signaled her crew to follow my car.

I took a right from the Ellisbridge Chaar Raasta and it took me less than five minutes to reach Shivam Stores, next to Hotel Shalimar.

Hari Bhai, the owner of Shivam stores came out of his grocery store to greet us as he saw a TV van descending on his mid-sized outlet. I had told DK last evening to inform the store about our plan, and he had done a good job in setting up things. The store looked much cleaner than the last time I had seen it on one of my market visits. The Uni-Cola crates were stocked neatly on the side and the refrigerator was stashed well with Uni-Cola bottles. Advertising material for the promotion was plastered all across the outlet and even the boys in the store were wearing white Uni-Cola T-shirts.

'You guys have done a fool-proof job here. Do not leave any stone un-turned to get maximum mileage. Even in a television story?' Bhavna commented after full seven minutes.

'What to do? The market place is so competitive; do not get many opportunities like this when a top channel like News Plus does a story on us. Have to grab the opportunity by the throat,' I force fitted Sumo's quote here.

'Yeah, yeah. No need to please me any further. I am committed to do the story now, Mr. Marketing Manager. Sunil, can you get the camera here please and start taking the owner bytes? We will do Chandan in the end,' Bhavna said organizing her crew and the shoot.

I stood aside for a while admiring her adeptness at the work and her smart managerial and organizing skills. Her attractiveness quotient seemed to be growing on me. My train of thoughts was put to a stop by Bhavna.

'Hey, we are done Chandan. Why don't you come here in front of this counter? We need to wrap this up fast, lights are fading,' Bhavna called me from inside the shop.

I sleepwalked on her instructions and finished my interview in about fifteen minutes. The television crew gathered their equipment and left. I offered to drop Bhavna back at the office and she agreed. I thanked Hari Bhai the owner and walked towards the car. Bhavna had already reached the car and was leaning on the front door.

'In a mood to have a cup of coffee with me?' I asked anxiously, fearing that she might refuse.

'Yeah, let us go to Kunaal opposite City Gold, I want to grab a sandwich too,' she said as if it was pre-decided that we would go there.

Kunal restaurant on Ashram Road was a youth hangout and served good enough fast food with a lot of variety. After parking the car and meandering through scores of motorcycles parked in front of the restaurant, we sat down. The restaurant was half empty and youngsters of different shapes, sizes and sex were scattered all around on multi-colored chairs. I ordered a coffee and sandwich for Bhavna and a Uni-Cola for my-self.

'Oh God, can you guys consume something that is healthy, aren't you tired of Uni-Cola Chandan? You could have had a coffee or a Nimbu-Paani either,' Bhavna said in a tone laced with mockery and despair and took a book out from her big brown leather bag.

'So what are you reading these days?' I asked, trying to switch the discussion subject from Chandan's unending devotion for Uni-Cola.

'Oh this one? Love in the Times of Cholera by Gabriel Garcia Marquez, have you read him?' she said as if asking me whether I had driven a Porsche.

'No, no I am not into all this heavy stuff. The maximum I do is newspapers and some heavily recommended business books. What is this one about?' I asked with the sole intention of taking the conversation further.

By now she was engrossed in the book and did not bother to look at me.

'It is about love, in its purest form', she said.

I looked around if I could find something more appealing than my partner, who had chosen to pose familiarity with an inanimate fable versus spending time with an interesting and well to do gentleman. People were segregated in groups of twos, threes and more but all of them were talking to each other except the two of us sitting within our own private spaces.

'Is the book so interesting Bhavna that you can't stay away from it even in a busy restaurant like this? What's the big deal about love and that too in this book?' I asked with a mixed feeling of intrigue and irritation.

Finally the lady looked up and chuckled, 'No point. An amateur like you won't get it. Let it be Chandan.'

I left her at Akash Deep building at 6.45. We did not speak much over coffee and sandwiches and just exchanged some basic pleasantries.

'Should I ask her out once at least?' I wondered.

She got out of the car and thanked me for the coffee.

'Hey it is nothing Bhavna, you are welcome. I am actually grateful to you for doing such a good story on our promotion. Thanks,' I said.

'Come on man! Say something Chandan, she is going. If you do not say anything today you lose your chance. Then you can rest peacefully in your two bedroom bachelor pad at Navyug. Say, say, say something for God's sake?' words emerging from my heart were pounding in my head.

'See you Chandan. Good Bye. Hope you like the story,' Bhavna said and walked away.

I moved the car a bit ahead and kept looking at her from behind an old tree. In a couple of minutes she melted amongst people entering the building. I felt like an idiot who gave it all away. I was completely oblivious to the environment as I drove my car. Was I numb? I was at Vijay Chaar Raasta when the ringtone shook me up.

It was Bhavna, 'Hey Chandan, I wanted to watch this movie *Makdee*. Will you come to watch it with me this Friday 7 PM show?'

I felt like someone who had just been granted a new lease of life after being sentenced to death.

Words failed me again as I said something stupid, '*Makdee,* but isn't that a kiddies movie?'

Bhavna chuckled, 'Yeah that is the reason that I am going with you. 7 PM on Friday and don't be late,' she said and hung up.

I parked my car on the side, leaned on the front door and gasped for breath while looking at the sky. Shahanawaz Khan, the bollywood superstar was smiling at me from a Uni-Cola hoarding on Vijay Chaar Raasta.

'Why can't men express what they are feeling most of the time? And especially you Chandan, for you communication can easily happen through sign language.' Bhavna said.

I stood silently for a moment before replying, 'Frankly somewhere within I am scared of rejection. It is better to keep quiet than to open your mouth and feel worse.'

She turned my statement on its head, 'It's better to be rejected earlier than being under the wrong impression for a longer time.'

I knew she was far better than me in using the right words at all times.

7
Unexpected Encounters

Unexpected joy and four large pegs of smuggled Royal Challenge whiskey at night had left me de-hydrated in the morning. I had to literally push myself out of bed at 8AM so that I could hit Baroda by noon. The critical task of getting dance girls for sales team motivational *massage* was still un-accomplished with only nine days to go. I had to hurry up my act. A dehydrated body and a throbbing headache could not rob me of my new found happiness of a blossoming friendship with Bhavna. I had a new driver from today, Kamal. He was in his mid twenties, married and already a father of two kids. His right cheek was perpetually swollen as it housed one full packet of *gutka* all 24 hours of the day. Such inflated cheeks were a common sight in Gujarat and I presumed that eating paan (betel) or *gutka* was a common trend here. Kamal was a lanky fellow with a bit of mischief in his eyes and I could sense that he was a bit reckless on the road.

'So how do you drive Kamal, fast or cautiously?' I asked him, realizing that it was a stupid question.

Equally scary was his answer, 'The way you would want me to drive sir. I can get you to Baroda in one and a half hours also.'

'I am in no hurry, just drive carefully,' I told him a bit unnerved.

It was 9.30 already and I had to pick up B2, my conduit for the mission.

B2 was waiting for me at Satellite Chaar Raasta, and waved at the car as soon as he saw my white Maruti zeroing at the signal.

'Good Morning Boss, I was just going to call you, I have been waiting here for more than forty five minutes,' B2 said as he got into my car hurriedly.

'Oh sorry man, had to make some important calls, could not do that later,' the manager in me lied cheekily.

B2 looked at me with his drunken eyes and a dumb face.

'So what is the plan B2, how are we finalizing the girls? Hope you have arranged for everything in Baroda?' I said as if I had asked him to get some chicken burgers from McDonalds.

'Yeah Boss, Jehan is waiting for us in Baroda. We will meet him at twelve in Hotel Holiday Inn; he has found out of a group of bar dancers who work in some Mumbai dance bar, Andheri East area, but belong to Baroda. Luckily they are in Baroda currently and have tentatively agreed to come to Ahmedabad. We have to go today and short-list four of them and also hand over the token amount. I have asked Jehan to do that for us,' B2 said with a tone oozing confidence.

After getting this assurance from B2, I could just slump into my comfort zone with Bhavna for the next two hours.

We crossed the TUCC plant at around 10am. The plant looked majestic like a palace and the parked Tata 407's reminded me of chariots in the olden times.

'Boss, sales are not picking up isn't it? Even TACC guys at the City Gold meeting the other day, were mentioning that they are negative against their targets,' B2 said in a concerned manner as if he would take a salary cut if TUCC Gujarat did not achieve its sales numbers.

I woke up after we had crossed Anand.

'How far is Baroda from here?' I asked.

It was my first visit to Baroda and the surroundings were not familiar. The first visit of a marketing head and that too for hunting down some raunchy women! I felt sorry at my situation once again.

'So you see B2, what all one has to go through in a marketing job? Shitty and tough but someone has to do it,' I said as if explaining some profound secret about universe.

B2 nodded his head like an innocent lamb.

We reached Hotel Holiday Inn on Old Padra Road in Baroda at 12.15. Jehan was waiting for us in the lobby. He was a glowsign and merchandise supplier for TUCC in Gujarat who had done reasonably well for himself in a short while. With no lineage or experience in this industry he had established a name for himself through sheer hard work, superior service and going an extra mile for his clients. Getting dance girls was a shining example of his relationship building skills.

"Sir you need not worry, I have checked out those girls. They are awesome lookers and performers. Your gujju sales executives will forget their wives and girlfriends; they will blindly accept the sales targets,' Jehan exclaimed in an assuring tone while we helped ourselves to an early lunch in the coffee shop.

'I hope so Jehan; let us finish that off fast. I need to leave for Ahmedabad by 4 pm,' I said wondering about how our encounter with these women would turn out.

'Where do these girls stay? Where are we going?' I asked.

'Fatehganj,' Jehan said chomping on his club sandwich.

We reached CJ block in Fatehganj in about thirty minutes. The narrow street was lined with single and double storied houses on both sides of the road. We stopped our car in front of one of the mud colored double storey house. The house looked absolutely inconspicuous from outside showing hardly any signs of sheltering dancing queens. Jehan knocked on a door on the second floor, while I looked around nervously. An old Gujarati sari clad lady opened the door. 'Kem chho Urmila Ben? (How are you sister Urmila),' Jehan greeted her. She nodded wryly and indicated us to follow her. We entered a room that only had a television set and a mattress on the floor. The lady asked Jehan to sit on the mattress; we followed her instructions as if in a trance. About ten minutes passed when a battalion of six women entered the room and stood in front of us, each striking a different pose like professional models.

'Sir aren't all of them great? Please select fast, I know it will be the most difficult choice to make,' Jehan chuckled.

It was an extraordinaire situation, and my brain was taking time to react. Hesitatingly I looked up and glanced at the six smiling faces staring at me with simulated lust.

'Yes all of them could fit the bill of an item girl,' I thought to myself.

Suddenly a racy bollywood song started playing from somewhere and the women started gyrating to it. Both Jehan and B2 were enjoying the exotic environment while I felt quite claustrophobic sitting in that room and watching an unreal and trashy performance.

Their dance stopped after five minutes and they rearranged themselves in exactly the same model like manner. 'Well these four are fine,' I said while pointing towards four of them in an animated manner as if picking up cattle from a village mela. The other two who had been left out looked at me in disdain for rejecting them. All of them left the room immediately but not before the 'selected' ones blew flying kisses at us.B2's excitement, all this while signaled to me a unique sales motivational experience lurking ahead.

Jehan summed up, 'So we will pick the girls up at 5 pm on coming Saturday, in two Sumos. They will be back early morning on Sunday. Fine Urmila *Ben*?'

She nodded, 'Ok fine, but ensure that the girls are safe and nobody misbehaves with them. It is your responsibility Jehan; I am sending the girls, only on your assurance. Pradeep will also go with you, and I need my advance now,' she said.

Jehan nodded, 'Oh sure Urmila Ben, your girls will be safe with me. Do not worry at all. My responsibility! And here is your advance.'

A bundle of Rs.100 currency changed hands. We came out of the house and that weird ambience in a few minutes.

While sitting in the car Jehan mentioned excitedly, 'Mathur sir, hope you liked the girls and all the arrangement.'

I was more than delighted to put an end to a bizarre experience that was successful. I was happy to go back to Bhavna.

'Yeah Jehan, damn good job done. You will have to raise an alternate bill for all these expenses. B2, just help this guy out.'

Both of them smiled and nodded their heads.

I was driving the car now after taking the wheel from driver Kamal who was sitting on the back seat and happily chewing on his gutka. B2 was sitting next to me. We were on the highway by 5 pm and I was already touching hundred on the speedometer.

'Good week Mr. Mathur, a hopefully successful consumer promotion, good advertising and PR, some brownie points from the boss and above all Bhavna,' I thought and a smile played on my lips.

The highway was not busy at all and I could see the *rabaris* goading their cattle back to the village as the sun set.

'Good job done B2 and that too quickly. As I was saying earlier, marketing job in a company like ours can pose various challenges and the smart ones always overcome them,' I said in a preaching manner.

B2 responded uninterestedly, 'Boss, can I push up the volume, I like this song.'

I nodded my head positively. Yeh vaada raha *(This is a promise)* re-mixed by DJ Aqueel played at full volume in the car. I could see the orgasmic effect of music on both B2's and my driver Kamal's face, their eyes were closed.

'Boss.....careful,' B2 shouted as I pushed my foot on the brake pedal with force and desperately tried to save my car from hitting the sheep that had suddenly run on to the highway.

With a loud thud the left hand side of the vehicle hit the sheep and the car screeched further before coming to a grinding halt. For a few moments there was silence, all of us being too shocked to react. Kamal was the first one to gain his senses and look back, the sheep lay motionless on the road. My head was throbbing and I could feel a stream of blood gushing in my veins. I looked back nervously and while doing that could see horror written boldly on B2's face.

'What happened is it alive? I am sure the car did not hit it with great force. Should we get down and see the animal?' I muttered, unaware of what was I saying.

'No boss no…these *rabaris* will screw our happiness. Let's get the fuck out of here. They are dangerous people, first they will take a lot of money, beat us up and might also burn the vehicle,' B2 said in a voice dripping with hopelessness.

'But isn't that stupid, I mean running away, they might just complain to the cops or come after us?' I again commented ignorantly and looked back.

A group of five to six *rabaris* were running towards the animal lying on the road.

'No boss we are neither Rambo nor Gandhi, let us just get the fuck out of here. Kamal you take the wheel and drive,' B2 ordered and took charge of the situation.

Kamal being the son of Gujarat himself, understood B2 completely, jumped out of the car and opened the driver's door. I pushed myself out of the driver's seat and resigned myself to sit at the back unwillingly.

'Get going man, just drive the car at full speed,' B2 shouted as Kamal turned on the ignition and sped off.

I turned back and saw the anger on the faces of *rabaris*, who had by now picked up the body of the sheep. The sheep moved and I heaved an instantaneous sigh of relief.

'See it is moving it did not die,' I exclaimed.

No one in the car seemed to be interested in whether the animal survived; they were more worried about their own survival. The car was growing its distance with the *rabaris*. I looked back again, they seemed to be angry and had started shouting, a couple of them started running towards the car, their faces colored with rage.

'Come on Kamal, faster, these ass holes will not leave us if they get us,' B2 was pepping up Kamal as if he was participating in a Grand Prix.

I turned back again and could see a tempo approaching the *rabaris,* they were signaling it to stop.

'They will follow us Kamal, go fast man, they have got a vehicle to follow us now,' B2 said in a crying voice.

I closed my eyes and the only words that resounded in my ears were 'Fast, Kamal fast.' The speedometer was touching one hundred and twenty; I looked back again to see the tempo at a good enough distance that was growing every minute.

There was no sign of angry *rabaris* and the tempo after some time.

Kamal heaved a sigh of relief, 'We just got saved today sir. Had it been a faster vehicle like a Sumo or something we would have had it. That tempo was bloody slow.'

I did not say anything. B2 got down at Satellite Chaar Raasta and walked to the front of the car, 'Its badly damaged boss, the left side is gone. You will have to leave it in the garage for at-least four –five days.'

I was too disinterested and shaken up to get out and measure the damage. Kamal dropped me at Navyug and left. I dragged myself to my two bedroom apartment waiting for me in darkness. The image of the lamb lying motionless on the road lingered in my mind for a long time.

'So what am I supposed to do, go out on streets and shout justice for

him? Or come to your channel and give a statement about who killed him? What should I do god dammit when I am not too sure about the truth myself?' I reacted emotionally.

Bhavna latched the door and sat on one of the chairs.

8
Makdee's Web

I was waiting for this morning. It was Friday and meant to be my movie date with Bhavna. I felt like an eighteen year old as I got up, similar excitement, nervousness and rush of blood. Yesterday had been a mixed bag, vacillating between emotions ranging from anxiousness and joy to pain and fear. But today appeared to be promising.

Bhavna did not call and it was 2pm already. I was wondering whether she had casually forgotten about it whereas I had been counting hours and minutes.

'I am not going to call her up, she should remember the plan if she has made it. Why should I call her?' I told myself.

At 5.30pm my patience gave up and I dialed her number. Before I could speak Bhavna's voice chirped, 'Hey how are you? What time are you picking me up? I hope you remember the plan?'

The pent up anger within me melted instantly, 'Hello! Madam you made the plan and you are supposed to confirm it,' I said complainingly.

'Oh I am so sorry Chandan. Tell me what time will you pick me up from the office? Let us watch it at City Gold,' she said.

'Arrey yaar my car has gone for repairs, just met with a small accident yesterday. I do not have a vehicle,' I said.

Bhavna was concerned, 'What happened? Are you all right? In that case you come straight to City Gold then and after the movie I can drop you home on my Scooty.'

Men love it when women show concern and care.

'Yeah, yeah all is fine. Just a small accident. Okay I will see you at City Gold at 7pm sharp,' and I hung up.

The multiplex was buzzing with people and energy at this hour.

'Where is Bhavna, it is just five minutes to seven?' I mumbled.

'Hello there! Come on let us go, I do not like missing the beginning of a movie,' Bhavna appeared almost running and grabbed me by the hand.

She bought the tickets in a jiffy and at seven we were comfortably ensconced in double cushioned seats of the multiplex. It was a good movie for kids and enjoyable for adults with some fine music.

We came out at 9.15pm, Bhavna was humming a song from the movie, 'Raat aye toh raat se darti hoon, meri maayi ri (I get scared when the night comes, Oh mother!).Beautifully sung nah and poignant lyrics. What do you say Chandan?' I nodded in agreement.

'I am feeling hungry; can we grab at bite a McDonalds before you drop me?' I asked. McDonald's was on the ground floor of the multiplex and had opened about four months back. Being the first one in Gujarat it had attracted enough media attention to have a separate vegetarian kitchen for the touchy vegetarian Gujarati consumer. Even at this hour it was almost packed with Gujarati's feasting on vegetarian burgers, Uni-Cola and french-fries. We sat on a table overlooking Ashram road with two Mc-chicken burgers and Uni-Colas.

'So are you married or still single?' she asked as she chomped on her burger.

'If I was married I would not be out with you at this hour alone, I guess,' I said a bit irritated.

'Well it does not matter to me though. We are out to watch a movie together. How does it matter what our marital status is?' she said.

'So where are you from Bhavna, what about your background and work life?' I asked as if interviewing a candidate.

'Me? Born in Nasik in a business family. Parents then moved to Mumbai, did my schooling and college from Mumbai and then post-graduation in mass communication. Worked in advertising agencies for four years and then joined News Plus. Dad has a furniture business, pretty extensive though. We have about five manufacturing units in Mumbai, he wanted me to do something in a similar field like interior designing etc. I said bull shit and moved here. Who wants to waste life in designing homes for other people? I would rather make a home for myself first. What say?' she looked at me with a question mark.

I was captivated with the way she talked and it took me a couple of seconds to react. 'Well yeah you are right. One must follow what the heart says. No point in getting trapped and follow a path that others think is right. My dad wanted me to be an engineer and here I am a marketer in a multinational FMCG. I failed my engineering entrance twice, not because of lack of interest but lack of study,' I laughed feebly.

'Do your parents stay with you? What about your family? Where are they?' Bhavna asked.

'Parents are settled in Lucknow. My education happened across various parts of North India, primarily Kanpur and Lucknow. So you can label me as a down to the core North Indian. In taste, thought and deed,' I said replicating my feeble laugh.

'Not a north Indian, but a *Lakhnawi* Bhaiyya,' she said and laughed loudly.

'So do you stay alone here? Why haven't you got married? You don't look that young? Clearly above the marriageable age in India,' she laughed again.

'Still haven't found the person I am looking for. I guess the search for my soul-mate ain't over yet,' I said as I looked into her eyes.

'So how, when and where are you going to find her Mr. Mathur? Hope this search does not continue for too long,' she said maintaining the eye contact.

'I will know it's her as soon as I see her. My heart will figure that out,' I said .

My lonely heart was itching to jump out of my chest, and confess on that red table, that she was the one. But it stayed put watching her eating the burger.

'So are you all by yourself here or do you stay with someone?' I said trying to encroach into her life now.

'Yeah, one of my dad's friends flat in satellite. It's a nice pad and I like going back to it after a day's work. Frankly I quite like being alone, contrary to what others may think. You know, in a traditional close knit Maharashtrian family, me staying alone and being un-married at twenty eight is everyone's favorite topic of discussion. But seriously Chandan, I love my privacy and space. When I am alone, I do not need to follow some rules or take care of someone; I just do what I want to at any point in time. If I want to read, sleep or watch television at a given moment I just do that, instinctively and no holds barred,' she said looking a bit lost in her own words.

'Don't tell me Bhavna that over your last twenty eight years on this planet you have not been able to find a single soul you could share your space with? I don't believe you?' I said.

'I said it is rare, not impossible. I had found someone who I thought I could share my space and life with,' she said.

My heart sank and I almost could not breathe.

I said feebly, 'See! So even you have someone. What is all that complaining about?'

'You feel worse when after hoping all the while that at-last you have found your soul-mate; you realize that he is not the one. Someone who you thought could match your values, your thoughts, your feelings and your character was just not the one you were waiting for. All that you kept chasing all this while was a dream,' she said and looked towards the delivery counter.

A serpentine queue led to the McDonalds delivery counter flocked with people and children running around in circles and repeating their snacking demands to their weary parents.

'So isn't he a part of your life anymore?' I probed.

'I wish he never was,' she said wryly.

'Do you want to tell me more?' I asked her instinctively.

I wanted to know more about this ass who could ever let go of a girl like Bhavna.

'Arjun Pingle used to be with me in school and then went on to do his engineering from IIT Bombay. Belonged to a lower middle class family and always studied through scholarships. I fell in love with him after school when he was going to study at IIT. We had similar interests and liked doing the same things. We remained very close even all through his electronics engineering days while I was doing my college. I had become a part of his life and always thought that our relationship would culminate into marriage. After graduating he got a job in US and went there on six month probation. My parents were initially quite wary of his family and all, but over time they realized that with a headstrong girl like me, they could never force their plans of a traditional marriage. We remained in constant touch for all those six months and planned to get engaged once he came back. He wanted to work for some time and give a decent financial stability to his family whereas I wanted to pursue my career in media journalism. I always thought that we understood each other so well that even a decision like this seemed so simple. For me it was a decision that came out of maturity and complete compatibility between two individuals. I respected and loved him for understanding me and my moral fiber. But while he had made a commitment with me, he was being pressurized by his parents for marriage within the same community. He always talked and laughed about it and said he would deal with it. I was so happy when he came back and wanted to get engaged and cement our relationship. One day he walked into a restaurant where I was waiting for him and told me that he just couldn't help it, he had to get married. His mother has stopped eating till the time he agrees to get married to a girl of her choice. He says that he loves me but can't hurt his parents who have raised him to reach here in life. When I ask him what about me? I have also waited for so long and let go of my youth and all those years just to be with him? He says that though he is getting married but he only loves me. This marriage is only for his family. He would continue to love me and would want to be in touch with me all his life. I walked out of the restaurant and our relationship that very moment,' she stopped and took a sip from the cola cup.

I did not know what to say, feeling sorry for her could have made her unhappy and being quiet would have meant I really did not care much.

'What hurt you the most Bhavna in this? Him walking out and breaking your trust or Arjun loving his family more than he loved you?' I thought I could do a post graduation in asking stupid questions.

Her eyes looked at me and I could see a touch of water in them.

'I hated myself for hurting me in the bargain. It was not Arjun, it was me who trusted him blindly and agreed to whatever he said. I was responsible for my actions and not Arjun or his family. I was hurt with my blind love for Arjun and believing in him more than I believed my heart and mind,' she said looking through the glass window.

'Did you meet him again? I am sure love doesn't diffuse so easily,' I said probing further. Why was I doing this, I hardly knew her that well?

'I lost respect for him after that. I guess respect for Arjun was a vital reason for someone like me, to be head over heels in love with. I just lost it completely. He tried to get in touch with me several times but I never responded, never felt like responding,' she said with an expressionless face.

I knew it was time to go.

'Its late 10.45, shouldn't we be going, you have to drop me too,' I said. Bhavna got up and we headed towards the two wheeler parking lot quietly.

'You wait here and I will go and get my scooty,' she said.

I saw her taking rapid steps towards the parking lot and wished I could do something to take away her pain.

'Let's go Chandan,' she said to me hiding behind an oversized helmet.

She looked as beautiful while sitting on that scooty as she did when she had entered my cabin at Thaltej. I walked towards the scooty and was extra careful while sitting on the back seat and keeping as much distance as I could, between us. There was a little bump ahead and unconsciously I had to hold her by the waist to maintain my balance.

I could feel our bodies quiver.

She was adept at everything. Even the way in which she drove the scooty had confidence and control epitomized.

'So here you are Chandan. Thank you for a good time and dinner,' she said as she took off her helmet in front of Navyug Apartments.

'Well I hope so. This guy also does not get to spend a time like this in such an interesting company often. So the pleasure is mine,' I said displaying my social skills.

'I will see you then, I hope I did not bore you with my stories. Actually you asked for it, I did not volunteer,' she said smiling at me as she put on her helmet.

'No not at all. I wanted to know about you and that is why I asked,' I said.

'And why do you want to know me, Chandan?' she asked.

'Um nothing I felt like, maybe you are an interesting person Bhavna. Can we meet again sometimes?' I said expectedly.

'Maybe? Depends on the reason and intent. What say?' and the scooty rolled.

'I will give you a good enough reason Bhavna, but let us meet again,' I said with a bit of desperation as I tried to catch up with that inanimate vehicle.

'We will, bye,' and she disappeared leaving me bewildered and longing.

9
Working On The Highway

The new week started today. I could not gather myself to call up Bhavna after Friday. I thought I had asked her too many questions, more than I should have, and she had opened up much more than she might have actually wanted to. I thought that our encounter that day at City Gold had left both of us a bit uncomfortable. I steered my thoughts towards other important tasks for the week, the TUCC consumer promotion and the sales motivation raunchy hungama on Saturday.

'Traveling up-country is a good idea to gauge how the promotion was faring,' I thought as I parked my car in Thaltej at the sales office.

I asked Maria if DK had arrived, knowing pretty well that her answer would be in the negative.

'When will this guy get it, that there is something called office timing?' I mumbled the umpteenth time.

After replying to all my mails and completing the weekly marketing report for Sumo, I stepped out of the cabin at11.30. DK was sitting with a supplier and giving him instructions about some new printing job for the TUCC promotion. Completely engrossed in detailing out specifications to the supplier, DK looked like concentration personified. 'DK meet me after you are finished with your meeting,' I said on my way to the loo.

DK looked back and nodded in affirmation.

I saw B2 entering the sales office as I came out of the washroom.

He was all sweaty and ruffled.

'What happened B2, you look pretty hassled?' I asked him.

'Boss, this Prashant Bhai from City One is a real ass hole, the proposal that we gave him, this guy showed it to TACC guys and asked them to improve it. What a bastard he is? And now he tells me today that competition has matched your proposal so get us a more lucrative deal?' B2 said with pure disgust.

'Do not bother too much. Just increase the overall deal by 10%. I have spoken to Sumo; we have five out of seven multiplexes in Ahmedabad. Even if we do not get this one, it is ok. We are not selling our souls for City One,' I pronounced judgment to B2 as I entered my cabin.

DK followed me into my cabin.

'Let's travel to Rajkot today DK and check out the impact of our promotion. Let us also take some on-ground feedback,' I said looking at my laptop screen knowing very well that an excuse was fast approaching. I was ready for it this time.

DK was visibly uncomfortable, 'Today? But boss I have lots to do plus some personal engagements also. Let us do it later.'

I assailed him with a pre-meditated reply, 'Sumo is planning to travel to Rajkot and wants to check out visibility for the consumer promotion. I am sure DK you would not want Sumo to be unhappy. Right?'

I was well aware, that one guy DK was shit scared of, was Sumo.

'Well, is Sumo boss coming? Ok fine let us go then. What time do we leave?' DK retracted from his earlier stance.

'Is the car looking fine, Kamal? I hope nothing is wrong now?' I double checked with Kamal if the garage guys had done a good job.

'Yes sir, there is no sound and dent is also completely gone. As smooth as butter sir,' Kamal replied while moving into the third gear.

DK was sitting next to me, silent and looking out of the window. *How unhappy the guy looks! Just because he has to travel out of the comfortable confines of his house for a couple of days. Laziness has crept in him with age.* I thought. We crossed Baola a small town on the Ahmedabad- Rajkot highway at 8.30. The highway was not crowded at this hour and a few private cars and trucks overtook us at regular intervals. Kamal was maintaining an average speed of seventy five to eighty.

'We should be in Rajkot by 12, what say DK? Courtesy these fantastic roads and less traffic,' I attempted to start a conversation with DK who was visibly quiet that evening. 'Yeah, boss infrastructure is really top-class in Gujarat. Be it good roads or twenty four hour electricity, even the smallest of towns will have it in abundance. Quite unlike other states, especially there up-north,' DK said with his gaze fixed on passing glow-signs fixed across the highway dhabas.

I had been a witness to Gujarat's infrastructure brilliance over last few weeks and could not deny this point, 'Yeah you are right, North India is not even a close second to it. Even the capital of India, Delhi has power cuts for hours. While from the time that I have come to Ahmedabad, I haven't noticed electricity cut even once. A lot has to do with prosperity of the state I guess.'

'Care for a drink DK? I want to have one,' I said while pulling out my half filled bottle of Royal Challenge.

DK looked at me surprised as if I wanted him to do drugs.

'No boss, I am not too much of a drinker except at social gatherings;' he said.

'Arrey, have a few sips DK we will do CarOBar *(North Indian slang for drinking in a car- Bar in a car)*,' I said while mixing neat whiskey in a half filled water bottle.

The smell and sight of the concoction relaxed DK a bit, plus I guess he was not expecting this sort of informality from his twenty eight year old boss.

I took a sip from the bottle, 'Yeah, tastes good, a little mild though,' and I added some more whisky from the bottle into the water.

I took another big swig. 'Perfect now, have a sip,' and I passed the bottle to him.

A bit hesitatingly DK also sipped from the bottle as he looked at me. DK's face contorted as he gulped the highly potent liquid and passed the bottle to me like a baton.

'Pretty strong boss, I do not want to have more,' he said.

'Mr. Sanyal, the first sign of a good whiskey is that the first sip hits you the most. Then onwards its smooth sailing,' I plugged a self made proverb with confidence.

This ruffian drinking panache was a result of years of practice within hostels of Lucknow University. We always had abundance of people, cheap liquor and water but scarcity of utensils. Adversity gives rise to innovation; we started using water bottles between us and soon forgot what glasses looked like. I was repeating the act today which even a stalwart like DK was finding very novel. DK took a few sips after that from the bottle and soon his apprehension was giving way to serenity.

'Our visibility is good on the highway boss, isn't it?' DK turned his head towards me. 'Looks fine DK, but we need to enhance it on the way to our plant. TACC is gaining momentum there and it is a route strategically important. Everyone takes it,' I said like a discerning manager.

DK looked at me as if I was a lunatic who was giving him directions to Baroda when he wanted to go to Rajkot. He merely nodded. It was about ten and we had finished about one and a half bottles of that heady cocktail.

'Should we stop somewhere for food? I am hungry, and let us give a break to the driver too,' I said in a fatigued voice.

'Let's stop at Savera Restaurant in Chotila, it serves good food and is also a TUCC exclusive account,' DK said with his eyes closed.

'Can this yester year superstar also perform in today's age and time? Does he have the skill and aptitude? Or will he be doing the same thing till the time he retires?' I thought as I dozed off.

We had finished our dinner and Rajkot was about an hour away. DK was already snoring. Kamal thrust another packet of gutka into his half open mouth.

10
The Truth About DK

The hotel phone-alarm beeped at 6.30 am. I wanted to sleep more but had to drag myself out of the comfy bed in Hotel Royal Inn. The morning routes would start leaving the godown by 8am, so had to get going to reach there by that time.

Giri Bhai the proprietor of Shakti distributors was sitting in his small glass cabin and talking to someone animatedly on his mobile phone. He nodded and gestured us to sit on the two vacant chairs placed opposite. Fifty year old and frail looking, he looked like a typical Gujarati from all angles. His red teeth were a result of at-least twenty years of rigorous engagement with gutka, and were in complete contrast with his spotless white kurta and pyjamas. His conversation on the phone veered around state politics with various references to state ministers and couple of times to the chief minister himself. Giri Bhai was a powerful political animal. One of the most known names across business circles in Saurashtra, Giri Bhai was a respected and feared person. He had several other distributorships besides TUCC but his majority of time was spent in politics. He was also known to be a power broker and his contacts within the state machinery were phenomenal. TUCC used to take frequent favors from him in all local matters, and the top company officials were on first name basis as far as he was concerned. It was rumored that Sumo took his help to douse the distributor strike in Saurashtra last year and earned brownie points within the company. He was also known for his mercurial temper. A couple of years back a hapless TUCC accounts executive who did not know much about Giri Bhai, landed at his godown to collect twenty lac rupees outstanding towards his distributorship. An irritated Giri Bhai asked him to come later. The annoyed accountant threatened Giri Bhai that he would get his distributorship cancelled. Giri bhai got so angry that he caught hold of the accountant, got him beaten up and then held him captive in the godown for two days. The local sales manager of TUCC had to pacify Giri Bhai to get him released.

'DK Bhai *Tame Kem Chho*?' Giri Bhai hugged DK after finishing his call.

'I am fine Giri Bhai how is business and family? Your trucks have not left till eight. All well?' DK said in a slight admonishing tone.

I was surprised that DK had no qualms about Giri Bhai's reputation and was talking business as he would to any other distributor.

'Arrey DK Bhai do not get disturbed, they are just leaving. Some of the trucks are carrying additional stocks today because of bigger orders that is why. They will leave in a moment. You relax and have a cup of tea. Who is this gentleman with you?' he said looking at me.

DK turned towards me and said apologetically, 'I am so sorry. Giri Bhai he is Mathur Sir, I wrote about him in my e-mail to you. My boss and the Marketing Head of Gujarat.'

'Oh welcome to Rajkot Mathur Sahib,' Giri Bhai extended his hand towards me.

The tea arrived soon and I could see the trucks leaving the godown at a steady pace. DK's tonic had worked and that too on someone like Giri Bhai, I was pretty impressed.

'So Giri Bhai, how is the promotion doing in your area? Any

impact on daily sales? Has the Uni-Cola consumption increased over last month?' DK questioned the distributor in my style. I liked that.

'Well DK Bhai though it's a bit early but I am sure it will work. I have seen the ads on TV, and the company has done a good job. It will start doing well first in slightly more affluent areas where the impact of television is more and then filter down to other pockets. Although I think it would have been better if the promotion had happened a bit later in March or April. It would have been a bit hotter then,' Giri Bhai's reply was more logical and truthful than any other feedback that I had heard till date.

'You are right Giri Bhai, but the company is now looking at pushing Uni-Cola across the year. We are looking at a strategy to de-seasonalize the business or to put simply, find new ways and means to increase Uni Cola consumption all through the year rather than just summer,' I tried to make him understand through my board-room marketing jargon. 'Whatever sir, I just understand one thing. No point in pushing your product if the consumer does not want to drink it. You guys can discuss and hope for anything sitting in your office. The hypothesis gets tested ultimately in the market. I still think we could have done this promotion after a month or so. Anyways TUCC is a big company full of intelligent people like you and DK. I am a simple businessman sir, whatever the company says we will try our best. Would you guys like to go on the routes?' he asked us getting up from the chair.

Both of us got up too.

'Yeah sure! I would like to do the market today. Want to see our presence as well as the impact of promotion,' I said.

Giri Bhai looked at DK and smiled, 'Sure sahib, please go and see for yourself. DK Bhai you can go with Purab, I am sending Mathur sir with Suresh to Yagnik Road and Kalawad Road. I hope you are staying for the night. Let us meet over a few drinks and dinner in the evening. Right sir?' I nodded in confirmation.

DK walked towards a truck and climbed up tucking his oversized stomach in. I waited on the porch with Giri Bhai, for Suresh my route agent cum escort to arrive.

'Cheers Mathur Sahib on your first visit to Rajkot. Hope you liked the market and our distribution,' Giri Bhai said as he took a large sip of his whiskey.

We had decided to meet in DK's room and I was relaxed after a much needed shower on a really tiring day.

'Yeah, it was good Giri Bhai. The servicing levels are good but low impact of the promotion. Do you know the kind of money that TUCC is spending on the promotion?' I again started off like a tape-recorder.

'Mathur Sir, I told you in the morning, firstly it is too early to pronounce judgment and secondly I think the timing is not perfect, 'Giri Bhai said as if he was talking to a young and inexperienced bloke.

'Giri Bhai please do not call me sir, I am younger to you. Please call me Chandan. But there is less visibility in the market. We got to improve it fast. DK tomorrow morning you must run the merchandising training course once again for all the route agents,' I said maintaining eye contact with both the gentlemen.

Both of them looked at each other and sipped their drinks, ignoring my observation.

'Why do I get this feeling that even DK does not believe in this promotion?' I thought and shoved off the balance whiskey from my glass.

'So how are Prerna and Sumanti doing DK Bhai?' Giri Bhai asked in a slurred voice.

We were down three drinks each and I guess Giri Bhai was running ahead of us by one peg. We had discussed and dissected everything from state level politics to the TUCCs strategy in Rajkot over the last one and a half hours.

'They are fine, one of them is in first year of college now while the other one will be taking her class ten examinations,' DK said circling the glass in his hands.

'How are Bhabhi and Maaji?' Giri Bhai further enquired. I was a bit surprised that both of them knew each other so well.

'Neeru's condition is the same as before and maa is now eighty plus, her health is sliding down,' DK said looking up as if thinking about something deeply.

'What happened to your wife DK? Is she unwell?' I asked while popping a salted peanut into my mouth and attempting to be a part of their conversation.

'You do not know Mathur sir?' Giri Bhai addressed me as 'sir' once more.

I nodded in denial and feigned complete ignorance.

'She is suffering from paralysis below the waist for the last fifteen years and is completely bedridden. You have not told Mathur Sir about this DK? He is your boss after all. You haven't shared the most important part of your personal life with him that everyone knows?' Giri Bhai chided him.

I was a bit shocked to hear this and looked at DK wanting to know more. His eyes showed signs of moistness.

'Nothing boss, an old accident, some fifteen years back when I was posted at Rajkot in my last company . We were traveling towards this side of Gujarat only, on a motorbike from Rajkot to Sayla to visit one of our friends, all five of us, I, my wife Neeru, our two little daughters Prerna and Sumanti and my son Avinash. We got hit by a truck from behind and the vehicle was thrown some hundred feet away into a nearby field,' DK said as he closed his eyes.

His body seemed to be revisiting the pain. Giri Bhai looked moved too.

'My two daughters and I were safe and received some minor injuries but my wife was paralyzed for life. We could not save our only son Avinash, though we tried very hard. Giri Bhai was the one who came running from Rajkot, ferried us to the hospital in one of the Uni-Cola route trucks and helped us in receiving timely treatment. Otherwise even Neeru would not have been alive. We would have given everything to save Avinash if it was possible. But everything failed,' DK was crying like a baby and streams of tears were rolling down his cheeks.

Giri Bhai continued, 'He was a beautiful kid DK. Thank the lord for he granted you Avinash's presence for those five years and made your lives happier. Mathur sir, DK has single-handedly raised his family from that day with support from his mother. He has been both a mother and a father to his daughters and they have grown into wonderful girls.'

I was numb and did not know how to react so I asked him a stupid question.

'So how do you manage DK, how is it possible with you being the only one at home? You must be having a maid?' DK looked at me with his face full of tears.

'No sir, apart from being expensive, no maid these days takes care of a person who is half paralyzed. Who wants to get into the hassle of cleaning up not just the body dirt but everything else as well? No one wants to soil his hands for a few bucks. So my mother and I have divided work between us, she takes care of the kids and my wife during the day when I am out at work. She cooks lunch, takes care of my wife and sends my daughters for tuitions. I take over once I get back from work in the evenings by cooking dinner and buying necessary household stuff, I also help my daughters in their studies if I can. Though most of the times I can't, because it has become quite tough these days. In the mornings I help the maid in making their breakfast and lunch that they carry to school, then go and drop them there. Then I come back home, give a sponge bath to my wife and head straight to work. Unfortunately I get a bit late most of the time, though I try really hard not to,' DK stopped and attempted a feeble smile but could not control himself and broke down again into deep and hard sobs that penetrated my soul. Giri Bhai hugged him and while trying to console him, he himself started howling.

It was strange to see two grown ups crying in unison but it was equally strange for me to see one man being as moved at another's sadness and felt it as his own. None of us had dinner that night.

It was twelve thirty when I lied down on my bed that night. That evening haunted me till about three in the morning. At last the mystery of DK coming late to the office was solved, once and for all. I could not bear it any more and got up to weep bitterly on the soft cushioned bed at Royal Inn. I did cry for a long time.

'Yes I am a witness to it but you cannot push me to feel the same pain as much as his family, beyond a certain extent. We are all individuals leading different lives, in different circumstances and facing different problems,' I said mixing contorted logic with philosophy.

'But we are humans bonded together with a string of compassion. There is no point in being compassionate and not having courage to stand for what is right. Empty compassion is pointless. No point in feeling bad for the poor one legged beggar knocking on your car window wearing tattered clothes. Everyone does it. If you have the balls, get out of the car and help him and mind you not just help him by giving him money. But help him by making his life better from that moment is what I call compassion backed by courage. Do you have it in you Chandan?' she said looking at me..

I was scared.

11
Dancing Queens

I hated abandoning our plan of traveling to Bhuj the next day. Sumo had called early in the morning and expressed the desire of discussing a plan to revive sales figures on an immediate basis. His point of reference, the consumer promotion was not doing too well and we needed a plan to push up sales.

'But I am in the middle of a tour boss? Could we do this over the phone Sumo or after we come back? We are already in Rajkot and this is my first visit to Saurashtra. I do not want to dump the plan in the middle,' I asked him.

'Its better that we meet Chandan, I have a lot of other crucial things to discuss too,' Sumo said a bit firmly.

'Ok Sumo. Both of us will get back today and I will see you early in the evening, 4 pm at the plant,' I said in a frustrated voice.

I lay on the bed for next half an hour with my eyes closed. "At-least DK would get back home a day earlier. Let his life get that perk at-least."

The critical meeting with Sumo for which he made me return to Ahmedabad got over in thirty minutes. I met her at the Upper Crust restaurant in Vijay Chaar Rasta at 6.30pm. 'Hey where have you been over last few days? I was expecting you to at least call up after being so desperate to meet me the other day,' she said with a cheeky smile on her face.

She looked quite pretty in a white salwar kurta as she sat on the chair opposite me. Upper Crust was almost packed, as always. Being one of the very few restaurants that served non vegetarian goodies and fast food, it was a regular abode for the 'carnivores' of the city. I looked at her and volleyed a feeble smile.

'What's wrong with you, you look drained,' she showed concern.

'Drained of emotions,' and I told her everything that had happened to me over the last two days. From rediscovering DK to sheer helplessness while dealing with my boss. Once in so many years, I had someone listening to me.

Our chicken rolls had arrived and we had them quietly without exchanging any words. I was feeling much lighter and relaxed.

'What are you doing on Sunday? Can we meet on that day? I am free the whole day,' I said.

She thought for a moment and said, 'Cool why don't we do this, lets go to Sabarmati Ashram, in the morning, come home and have lunch with a couple of beers. What say?'

'Sounds good! Beer after a visit to Sabarmati, a bit anomalous though but works,' I said gladly.

'Isn't life peculiar? Here you were sitting with a long face half an hour back and now you smile at the prospect of going out with a sexy and charming lass on Sunday,' she said. The lady was sexy and good with words.

'Yeah that is true man. Let's go. I need to go to Thaltej office for a while. I look forward to Sunday Bhavna,' I said and got up.

'Can I ask you something?' she said as she got up and followed me out of the restaurant. I nodded my head.

'Why do you have to agree with your boss all the time, when you know that he is wrong?' she asked.

'Because I give him the benefit of doubt. Ha! You just can't keep fighting with your boss forever. To reach a consensus you need to give in a few times as well,' I tried to push reason into the talk.

'But is it fair that you end up losing most of the times? That is a screwed up philosophy,' she said coldly.

Darkness had set in and I was unable to see her scooty after a few seconds. "I think I love her" I muttered to myself and told Kamal to drive towards Thaltej.

'B2 is every thing in place for today?' I stroked him in a friendly manner while entering my cabin.

It was Saturday today. Our date with the dancing queens. He stared back at me with his drowsy eyes.

'Where were you boss? Have not seen you for ages. Yeah every thing is fine boss; spoke with Jehan in the morning. We are going as per the decided plan. I have also arranged for the set up at Greenwood Resorts with a small stage and sound. We can see that slightly early in the evening if you want to. Sales team will start arriving in Ahmedabad from the afternoon today,' B2 replied in a confident voice.

I could sense that he was in control and that gave me a lot of comfort. A task like this was not just tough but peculiar as well. I was a bit uncomfortable in taking it up but these guys just made it happen with so much ease.

'I hope things go off well today and the sales team is just bloody happy. That is the only outcome I want from this stupidity,' I thought as I clicked on my Inbox.

'Should we move towards Greenwood boss? The sales team from Surat has already arrived and the rest are coming in from other areas as well. I have intimated them to reach the resort by 8pm,' B2's head popped into my cabin.

I nodded and fifteen minutes later we were speeding towards Gandhinagar.

'I hope this is completely safe and discreet B2,' I said looking at him.

'Boss do not worry, I have spoken personally to the owner about it. He is an old hand at it, *puraana paapi hai* boss,' he said with mischief in his eyes.

'And what time does the party end?' I asked resting my head on the back-seat.

'Looking at finishing it off by twelve latest. The guys would have had an overdose of liquor and women by then,' he said and laughed sinfully.

I closed my eyes thinking about what would unfurl in the evening today. The drive to Greenwood was mixed with anticipation and fear of the unknown.

'Everything looks fine here B2, hope Jehan and the girls are on their way,' I said looking at him.

B2 looked at his watch; it was 7PM. 'Yeah boss, everything is on track. Jehan is on his way with the girls. They should reach Anand in another fifteen-twenty minutes, I just spoke to him,' he said.

The arrangement at Greenwood Resorts looked good. The resort was spread out in acres with a water amusement park on one side and a few rooms and a couple of medium sized conference halls on the other. Amusement parks were the latest fad in Gujarat and drew huge crowds on weekends. The rooms were rented mostly by wealthy Gujaratis coming over from neighboring small towns and spending weekends with their families. They were also put to use quite effectively for a weekend rendezvous by adventurous un-married couples. Besides family visits a lot of private companies had started holding their quarterly conferences and distributor meets at these resorts. But our get-together was exceptional. Sales guys had started trickling into the hall that we had rented for our get-together. Sumo had told me specifically not to disclose the agenda and the act that we were putting together for the sales team, but to dazzle them with the un- expected. 'Chandan, let us give them the unexpected, let us surprise them and delight them so much that they commit to sales numbers and then achieve them anyhow,' Sumo said. I looked at the bar-counter adorned with various liquor bottles and Uni-Cola assortments. The waiters had started with their round of snacks. The sales teams had divided themselves into groups and were busy discussing their market and sales issues and seemed eager to unfurl the mystery behind the evening get-together. Occasionally a sales manager or an executive would come up to me and try to inquire about the agenda. My lips were sealed.

B2 came to me and hushed, 'They have just entered the resort; I have asked Jehan to take them to the rooms at the back of this hall, where we have made arrangements for them to freshen up and get dressed etc.I am going there to ensure that they do that quickly. Do you also want to come boss?' I knew that the real action would not start before Sumo arrived.

'Let's go,' I said as I followed B2 in the darkness.

'Jehan, all set for the evening and a rocking performance?' B2 said while entering the room.

'Yeah, Yeah B2 brother all will be fine, don't you worry. Your sales team will fall at your feet after they witness this extravaganza,' Jehan said flicking his hair.

The girls were crouched on sofa and chairs in the room and gave us a simulated lusty look that I ignored.

'Ok, you guys dress up fast, we are waiting for Sumo boss to come in the next ten minutes. All of them should be ready to hit the stage in half an hour. Jehan, I will give you a missed call as a signal to come into the hall, Ok?' B2 spoke like a Bollywood director.

We walked back towards the hall. 'Hope everything turns out fine,' I muttered in the darkness. B2 was confident, 'Boss don't you worry.'

I saw Sumo standing in the centre of the hall like an emperor looking all around. Occasionally he would glance at his unsure subjects. His smile when he saw me was unnerving. The emperor seemed to be pleased.

'The arrangement is quite good Chandan, have the girls come? I hope no one here knows about our real plan,' Sumo chuckled excitedly.

'Sumo do not worry, no one knows about it. Everything is as per the plan and the girls have arrived. They are in the room, getting ready,' I said with some borrowed confidence from B2.

Sumo looked at me admiringly. I was the one shaping his obnoxious dream into a reality. 'I think we should start Sumo, why don't you start with a short speech and set the ball rolling? I will signal the girls immediately to start with a bang. The guys out here will be taken by surprise,' I said.

For the first time Sumo seemed a bit nervous.

'So now our man seems to be getting psyched with the dancing queens huh! Till now it was only within the head but soon it is going to be a bawdy reality and that is a bit scary, isn't it Mr. Sumanto Sen? However successful it may be, in my eyes it will always be meaningless and vulgar. I will never feel good about it,' I muttered angrily.

Sumo said in a low voice, 'No, I think you should go on to the stage first Chandan. Call me up in two minutes and I will kick-start the evening. From then on you guys take over the evening. I don't think I will be sticking around for long,' I nodded in affirmative.

After a brief talk on the ongoing consumer promotion and up-coming marketing plans to boost sales in the summers, I invited Sumo on the stage. He looked positively tense. 'Friends, today's evening is organized to launch our mission for achieving the sales targets this summer. I am proud to be the head of such a talented team which I am sure will leave no stone unturned to convert this dream into reality. One more thing this team would be doing differently from all the previous years. Instead of just committing to achieve sales numbers this time, we would be signing a pledge, a bond right here, that would keep reminding us of our promise every single day from today,' Sumo's nervousness was giving way to an emotional outburst.

'Friends, Chandan and his team have put up a show today that is the first of its kind, an FMCG innovation in team motivation. Though the idea germinated here, in my mind but as a wise man has said, a great idea can die a natural death if not executed effectively. Good job done by the marketing team and a big round of applause for them! So my dear friends enjoy yourselves, make merry but do not forget the promise that each one of you will make today. Even if you guys try to, I will not let you. So have fun,' Sumo glanced at each one of the hundred odd guinea pigs who were experiencing the motivational extravaganza, all getting ready for the slaughter.

There was silence in the room for a few seconds, perhaps the guys were trying to figure out what Sumo exactly meant, but then with tempting liquor around and the promise of a wild night who wanted to wrack their brains. A thunderous applause broke out with everyone looking at the marketing people with admiration, responding to Sumo's acknowledgement. I felt like a sleazy film producer in Bollywood and squirmed in my space, B2 seemed elated like a celebrity.

The stage dazzled as B2 signaled the girls to come up. Amidst smoke and flickering lights the divas descended on this very earth and smashed my poor, famished sales team out of their wits. Even in the wildest of their dreams, those Gujjus could never imagine that they would be treated to this deadly combination of intoxicating whiskey and seductive women. The girls were gyrating wildly to the beat of one of the hottest song in the current disco circuit.....*Na Ugli Hi Jaye Na Nigli hi jaye, ye kaali zehreeli raat. Pal pal balkhati pal pal ujlaatai, palke jhapakti yeh raat*(*It isn't possible to either leave or embrace this dark and poisonous night. This alive and breathing night is changing its color every passing moment*).

'What a pertinent number for this night!' I thought as I poured my third peg. Sumo was thoughtful standing next to me and admiring his poor subjects being devoured by the storm of unadulterated gratification.

As liquor started flowing in the veins of the men, their admiration started taking different bearings. From dancing around the girls in circles, their bodies enacting lewd gestures, a few of them became more passionate and started touching and pulling a couple of them into their arms. The girls had seen and balanced such situations in the past a number of times. A magnitude of uncouth and unruly customers with pockets full of currency! They were experts at emptying such pockets while massaging their manly inflated egos. The boys were eating from their adept hands and swinging to their tunes in no time. Matching step with step and move with move it was sheer male rhapsody at public display. Smoke coming out of the machine at regular intervals and armed with an array of lights had turned the entire atmosphere completely stimulating and we were engulfed in it, being sucked deeper and deeper.

'When do we start rounding off the evening, and get the pledge sign off from the boys?' my trance was broken by Sumo's words.

'Yeah let us do it now, it's close to eleven thirty already,' I said getting up.

As I signaled for the music to stop, the boys looked really pissed for cutting short their jamboree. The girls heaved a sigh of relief on retrieving freedom from an unruly mob getting dangerous with each passing minute. All of them immediately lined up next to me on the stage.

Sumo appeared from nowhere on the stage with a bundle of printouts like Phantom from the forests of Bangalla.

'So boys after this wonderful and unforgettable night, now comes the time of reckoning for us to take an oath like true men who live up to their promise. A promise that is to achieve the sales targets for this quarter and today we will make this promise, in front of these lovely ladies who have turned this night into a truly memorable one. All the sales managers and team heads need to come on to the stage one by one and sign off this commitment of sales numbers. Guys, if we live up to our oath, I promise you that these ladies will return after three months, here with all of you, again,' Sumo ended his whiskey laden speech. I shuddered with the thought of doing an encore performance after three months.

The circus started thereafter. Each sales manager and team head came up on to the stage and signed a piece of paper that had his team target written on it and then handed it to the girl of his choice. The girl that he would choose would walk up to him seductively, take his goddamn pledge, shake his hand and wave to the crowd like a diva. The crowd would reciprocate with whistles and lewd cheers. This unabashed display of idiocy continued for next half hour with all of us as meek spectators. Sumo grinned from ear to ear. Half drunken comrades of TUCC Gujarat started gobbling the food somehow and leaving. A few of them were enquiring about the girls' whereabouts hoping to continue with their recently acquired friendship. But the girls had disappeared with Jehan almost thirty minutes back into darkness that would lead them to Baroda. I was pretty sure that if not the sales targets and Sumo, the girl's at-least would haunt the memories of this bunch of guys for the next quarter.

'Hey Chandan, that was a good show man. I never thought that you guys would be able to pull this off in less than two weeks and that too with such professional dancers. I think the guys were very happy and charged for achieving their targets. What say?' Sumo said while walking back with me towards the car park. I could sense that both of us were a bit tipsy.

'Yeah even I was tentative to start with, B2 did a great job in organizing things,' I said unlocking my car.

Sumo's driver was waiting for him with the Maruti Esteem door open. With half his body inside, he stopped, 'So what do you think. Was today motivating enough for these guys to get us out targets?'

I wanted to shout NO with all my strength.

'I hope so Sumo, looks like the guys are excited,' is actually what I said.

Sumo smiled, nodded his head and sped away.

Kamal smiled at me mischievously as I surrendered on the back seat of the car.

'What a party sir, even I managed to look at those girls from one of the corners. God fun and what girls?' he said as if talking to his friend in a dance bar.

I looked up and gave him a stern look. He kept quiet till we reached home.

'Bhavna you guys were in my office premises. Do you know how media shy these MNCs are? My boss was so worried about media landing up at our office. He was fucking on my head. I had no other alternative but to drive you guys out by hook or by crook,' I pleaded. More silence prevailed and neither of us moved from our places.

12 Confession At Sabarmati

A drizzly morning awaited me after a long and momentous night. The sheer excitement of spending the whole day with Bhavna robbed me of my early morning sleep and I was up by 7 am. I switched on the television and half interestedly flicked through the fifteen odd news channels. Nothing on the tube could hold my interest with everyone covering the launch of a Yatra called by a national political party, to mobilize Hindus for the construction of the Ram temple at the highly disputable site of the Ram Mandir at Ayodhya. With nothing else to kill time with, I continued watching the idiot box for a while.

I was there at Bhavna's building by 10.30 sharp. It being a Sunday, Kamal was on leave and I was driving myself. She was standing on the road in front of her building in a pink salwar suit and looking as endearing as always.

'So how have you been dude? What's happening?' she said while sitting next to me on the front seat of the car.

'You have got to really hear it to believe this Bhavna,' I said while changing over to second gear.

The next thirty minutes of the drive was filled with gory details about the wild Saturday night that I was a party to. I filled her up with the minutest details of the motivational circus that ensued right from the resort to the girls, from the pledges to the drunken ruckus. I found her looking at me agape when I took a left turn on the

Ashram Road to reach Old Vadaj where Gandhi Ashram was. The drizzle had settled down and the sky was giving way to the morning sunlight in a covetous manner.

We walked from the ashram parking on the stone laden pathway in silence.

'Have you been here before?' I asked her whilst absorbing the calm serenity of the place. 'Yeah, I think this is my fourth visit here. I quite like this place. Do you know that Gandhiji stayed here for good fifteen years after he came back to India from South Africa? This was the place where he shaped his philosophy and thoughts, about leading India to freedom,' Bhavna replied.

'But thousands of people contributed towards Independence. It was not just him?' I said. 'But his contribution perhaps was the maximum don't you think? Gandhiji stayed here from 1917 till 1930, the time when he led India to the famous Dandi Salt March,' she continued talking as she stopped in front of the red brick gallery of the Gandhi Smarak Sanghrahalaya or the Gandhi Museum.

We walked around the museum corridor joined with scarcely lit rooms lit with little sunlight seeping through the open windows. The painting gallery was adorned with hand drawn panels that depicted major events in Gandhi's life while he was in Ahmedabad. The exhibits were arranged neatly and chronologically talking about each of these events such as Swadeshi and the Champaran movement.

'Do you know what Nehru said about Gandhi in his tribute?' she said while continuing to walk. I shook my head.

'Wherever he trod became hallowed land. Wherever he sat became temples. This ashram is actually between a jail and a crematorium. Do you know why?' she said. I shook my head again.

'Well Gandhiji thought that a satyagrahi invariably has to go to one of these places. Originally this ashram was called the *Satyagraha Ashram,* based on Satyagraha or passive resistance the philosophy that Gandhiji followed. The philosophy of non-violence through which Gandhi took India towards freedom,' her words echoed in the sparingly populated gallery.

There were hardly any visitors to the gallery that day, except an odd couple perhaps looking for some privacy and a family out for a Sunday picnic.

'Gandhi thought that this was the right place to carry out the search for truth. He walked on the land where you and I are standing right now,' Bhavna continued talking.

We spent about half an hour walking through the two galleries in the museum that offered all relevant information on major events from Gandhi's life. Bhavna seemed visibly excited of being there, even though it was her fourth visit. She actually pushed me into the museum book store despite my complaining that I had no interest in it. But she persisted. We left the museum and walked towards the centre of the ashram that housed a humble belonging.

'This is Hriday Kunj where he lived till the time he vacated this place. It was here that an ordinary mortal Mohandas Karamchand Gandhi turned into Mahatama Gandhi. In 1930 when the British government taxed the Indian salt to promote import of its own foreign salt, Gandhi opposed it and united the country with an awakening called The Dandi March. You would have heard that at-least. Thousands were put into jails and the government also forfeited their properties. Gandhi resisted this strongly and urged the government to seize his property as well. After the government did not oblige, he decided to leave the ashram and vowed never to return till India attained Independence. But Gandhi could never return, even after India got independence in 1947. He was assassinated in 1948,' Bhavna said softly while looking at the white cushion , a small wooden table and a charkha (spinning wheel) in the room adjacent to the courtyard of Hriday Kunj where Gandhi used to sit and meet all the guests from India and abroad.

I loved everything about her, intelligence, wit, her wise cracks and her intellect. The more I met her, talked to her and saw her, the more my love seemed to grow and now almost overflowing. I wanted to tell her this but was this the moment? I was perplexed. 'You have an alternate career option Bhavna. You can double up as a guide at the ashram. You seem to know so much,' I said satirically.

'Yeah a guide like me can only make money if I get ignorant people such as you coming here all the time,' she said flashing a smile. Bhavna never left an opportunity.

We drifted towards Upasana Mandir or the place of worship where Gandhi prayed everyday in the morning and the evening. It was close to twelve but the weather was good. The morning drizzle had turned Ahmedabad pleasant. The river lay in front of the ashram and Ahmedabad looked at us with sprawling modernity from the other side. The Mandir was surrounded by lush but old trees. The only audible sound was that of a thousand chirping birds. We closed our eyes to say a prayer. I looked at Bhavna, her eyes were closed perhaps assimilating every iota of spirituality within herself and her face looked serene and beautiful. A pure heart that prayed for something. I could not resist any further.

'Bhavna, I love you. It's too early though, but from the moment I saw you, I think I love you. I do not want you to react but I cannot hold it within me. Even though you may find it completely ill-timed but I just cannot fight this feeling anymore,' I said in a daze.

Her eyes were closed all the while I talked to her.

'Did you too dance with those women that night in your stupid party Chandan?' she asked me as she opened up her eyes and looked at me with mock anger. My eyes were fixed on the ground and I nodded my head in negative. She clasped my left hand and touched her heart with it.

I thought I had been hasty with my confession. We got up from there and made our way back through the gardens. Bhavna was quiet and that added to my confusion of what she thought of my ill-timed acknowledgement of love.

'So what do you like the most about Gandhi and this place?' I questioned knowing that she would at-least answer this one.

'He was a man who could stand up for what he thought was right. It is so difficult to do that Chandan. Did you read what was written in his own handwriting on the museum panel?' she looked at me.

'Umm...well there were many, I do not recall any one in particular,' I said trying to pick up the right one from my patchy memory span.

'My life is my message is what Gandhi had written. To me this is about supreme conviction that Gandhi had in the way he lived his life. He was an ordinary human being like us but he did what was right and what he believed in. That made all the difference. A man who can say that his life is his message? Wouldn't he be so confident that the life he led was so correct that it could be an inspiration for generations to come? For me Gandhi is an epitome of strength of character and that draws me towards him and his ashram. Frankly that draws me towards anyone who has it. You too have it Chandan, you are a good and honest man,' she gave me a loving look and held my hand. I held it tightly till we reached the parking lot to get into the car.

'You have a nice pad here lady!' I said as I glanced around her three bedroom apartment in Satellite.

It was one thirty in the afternoon and the sunlight was flowing quite freely into her living room. A look into the house and one could confirm that Bhavna was artistic. The chimes whistled in the balcony that led to the living room with low seating i.e. mattresses covered with ethnic sheets and a couple of low and armless chairs. Pictorial coffee books on the artisans of India and Indian Independence were laid on one side of the coffee colored table.

'Why can't men express what they are feeling most of the time? And especially you Chandan, for you communication can easily happen through sign language.' Bhavna said.

I stood silently for a moment before replying, 'Frankly somewhere within I am scared of rejection. It is better to keep quiet than to open your mouth and feel worse.'

She turned my statement on its head, 'It's better to be rejected earlier than being under the wrong impression for a longer time.'

I knew she was far better than me in using the right words at all times.

The walls were decked with a series of black and white framed pictures with abstract human forms. One of them showed two frail hands cupped together waiting for the rain drops to fall on them while the other had two toes touching one another against the backdrop of the sea. The pictures were in black and white and very distinct, matching with her personality and taste.

'Make yourself comfortable, and it would be good if you can take off your shoes in the rack near the door,' Bhavna said while dumping her bag on the small two-seater dining table next to the main door.

'What are we having? You had mentioned beer if I remember. Right?' I said and parked myself on one of the chairs.

'Yeah yeah, beers are there. What do you want to order for food?' she said as she handed over a glass of water to me.

It was getting hot and I was thirsty but I only had a couple of sips from the glass hoping to quench the balance thirst with a beer.

'Let's order some mutton biryani from Fraizer's. His is the only decent non-vegetarian joint in this part of the city,' I said picking up a book.

The sight of a chilled bottle of Kingfisher beer in the dry state of Gujarat soothed my gills. Bhavna took some in a small glass and handed over the rest of the bottle to me along with a beer mug.

'Aren't you going to take a little more?' I asked her while emptying the entire bottle into the mug.

'No, I am fine. I will take more if I want to. I don't feel like it,' she said in between her conversation with the restaurant.

'I hope that I am not to be blamed for spoiling your mood. I really did not want to hurry it up,' I said feeling like a convict.

'Arrey no baba seriously it's not you and my mood is not spoilt. Cheers,' she smiled and raised her glass for a toast.

We talked for some time about her family and her early days in Ahmedabad, her school, college and friends. I stayed away purposely from any conversation regarding Arjun. I had gulped down about a couple of beers by now and was a bit tipsy.

'Hey you cheap guy, you haven't taken off your shoes yet. Please,

please do Chandan,' she said to me. I made a face and walked towards the door.

'Chandan, you walk like a wrestler... why can't you walk normally?' Bhavna said.

'Arrey I do that more when I am feeling good,' I said.

'So pretentious you are, you bloody Bhaiyyaji,'she chuckled from behind.

I walked back and took my earlier position; Bhavna was sitting opposite me on the mattress and looking at me.

'So why do you love me Chandan?' she asked. I was not expecting the question in the first place and two bottles of spirit had further dampened my thinking.

I kept qu' . for a couple of minutes, 'Because you are extremely cocky and very attractive.

Bhavna burst out laughing, so much so that tears came out from her eyes.

Suddenly she went silent, 'I do not know whether I can love anymore, somewhere I feel I have dried up. That is why I did not answer you at the Gandhi ashram.'

'Oh I thought you did not want to lie in Gandhi Land by saying yes,' I replied instantly. She laughed again and got up. I got up too and held her hand, blocking her way to the kitchen.

'I mean it Bhavna and I will make sure that you love me as much as I do,' I said.

She said nothing and came closer to me. I held her by the waist and kissed her on the lips not just once but many times. The sudden spurt in passion was doused by the shrieking doorbell. The intruder was this ass from restaurant carrying the order.

Bhavna laid the food on her tiny dining table. I put some biryani in a plate and sat down on the chair.

'So what's your plan for the week?' I asked her while polishing off the last few drops of beer in the glass.

'I am going to Mumbai tomorrow, have a family wedding to attend to. Should be back by Thursday,' she said finishing off her helping.

'Oh, I will miss you. Will you call me?' I said candidly.

'Of course I will. The kiss will not let me forget you for next three days atleast,' she laughed again.

I didn't like her comment but I was happy because she was happy. It was time for me to leave and I did not like it.

'How is Anwar Bhai doing by the way?' she asked casually.

'I haven't seen him for quite some time but I guess he would be fine,' I replied while opening the door latch.

'I have not visited him, I need to do that soon,' she came closer to me and hugged me tight.

'See you man, take care and be good. Do not get into one of your evil parties again. I will keep a watch on you ok?' she said.

I nodded my head and walked towards the elevator. The sun was giving way to the evening and weather was still cool. I instinctively looked up at her flat on the fourth floor. She was out there in the balcony and gave me a huge grin as soon as our eyes met. I waved back.

'Oh Man! I love her!' I said to myself.

'You don't love me Chandan,' she said.

'Why? Who says so? Just because I have not told you this one thing that you expected me to tell you does not mean that I do not love you,' I argued with her.

'Knowing fully well that this was the only thing that I expected from you in our relationship, if you could not keep just this one promise of being truthful then you certainly don't love me. Why did you hurt me again Chandan? Why, after Arjun, you too did the same thing! Why??' she screamed and then started sobbing.

I was sitting on the same mattress where we had made love for the first time. I could not gather myself to get up and stop her from crying. I just sat there speechless.

13
City Under Siege

28th February shook Gujarat like an earthquake. I got up on Thursday morning anticipating a meeting with Bhavna, but came face to face with the dark side of humanity. A train carrying Hindu religious workers coming back from Ayodhya was allegedly set on fire by Muslims near Godhra in South Gujarat. The entire state was up in a blaze. The newspaper headlines screamed of widespread communal riots slowly spreading across the length and breadth of the land. A bit worried I called Bhavna on her mobile.

'Hi, good morning baby how is you?' I said.

She sounded groggy, 'Oh Good, just got up. What's happening there?? We spoke yesterday afternoon right? And till then there was nothing, but things seemed to have changed three sixty degrees over last twenty four hours and for the worse. I have been getting frantic calls from the office to return as soon as possible. I believe there are riots all across Ahmedabad, Vadodara and Northern parts of Gujarat. There is also a statewide strike today isn't it? Good that I had a back up in the office who is reporting from Ahmedabad otherwise, it would have been an issue for me. My head office has already sent a couple of correspondents in different parts of Gujarat to cover it in detail. Hope you are not venturing out James Bond?' she said.

'But why do you want to come here now Bhavna?? Please cancel your plans of coming to Ahmedabad now. The place is up shit creek.

Why can't you just stay put? The rest of your office gang can take care of it,' I said getting a bit panicky.

'Don't worry baby. I will take care of it myself. Please understand I am in the business of news and for that I need to be where it is happening. And as of now, Gujarat is on the centre of world news. So I have to be back, if not today then latest by tomorrow,' she said calmly.

'But it isn't safe Bhavna plus your locality Satellite is just on the border of a sensitive area. And you live alone. I am just worried,' I almost pleaded.

'Ok baby if you think it is so unsafe why don't you come and be with me to protect me?' she said in a flash. I was taken aback and it took me a while to react to the proposal. But I felt quite excited with the prospect of spending entire twenty four hours with Bhavna. 'Okay fine but I am not too sure whether you would be able to adjust with my erratic staying habits,' I said covering up my nervousness.

'It's my house and I set the rules. I will come in tomorrow morning and go straight to the office. You may come anytime in the evening,' she said.

'Bhavna parts of the city are under curfew, even I am not going to office. We are not plying the routes today and that means no TUCC trucks will go into the market. Trust me! This is uncommon Bhavna. So how will you go to the office?' I asked.

'There will be an office cab for me at the airport and I am a media professional. Believe me I will manage. This is the time for us guys to work. You take care and I will see you tomorrow,' she said and hung up.

My worry had given way to excitement of living with Bhavna. I had started counting hours.

The situation worsened by the next day. The state was under red alert and a majority of the city under curfew. Rumors were floating like innumerable farts in thin air. Bizarre incidents of violence, killing, arson, rape you name any atrocity under the sun, was getting reported. I had been trapped in my two bedroom jail for last couple of days and it had been tough. TUCC trucks were plying only on a few routes in New Ahmedabad and business was looking bleak in the near future. I had not been to the office for last couple of days and only working through my mobile phone and internet. Sumo's worry on his quarterly sales numbers that he had committed was palpable from his phone-calls. The sudden riots had distanced him further from the target and he looked really concerned. Trapped in my apartment, I was spending time watching television and in between talking to my team guys and sales managers from different parts of Gujarat. The state of affairs looked grim and business was doomed, at least for the coming month. The sight from the balcony was suffocating. Currents of thick black smoke emanated from different parts in the city. Even roads in a supposedly new and up-market area like Bodakdev had very few people. The shutters on the shops in the local market were down and an eerie silence pervaded. Ahmedabad looked dead and burning. I thought of visiting the Thaltej sales office before going to Bhavna's house in evening the next day.

The ever buzzing TUCC sales office was quiet. Eighty percent of the trucks were parked in the godown signaling hardly any vehicle movement or sales in the market. The office was devoid of any staff except Anwar Bhai behind his desk. He was engrossed in his work and a couple of agents were sitting across him and counting currency for settling day's accounts. Dakshesh's room was locked.

'Hello, Anwar Bhai. Isn't Dakshesh coming today?' I asked him politely respecting the bond he shared with Bhavna.

Anwar Bhai immediately stood up and greeted me, 'No sir, he is not coming today. Called me up about an hour back and asked me to shut the office after all the settlements.'

'Oh, how are sales? I am sure they are badly affected. How many routes did we run today?" I asked.

'Arrey sir do not ask. It's very bad. We are doing only twenty percent of what we would be doing on a normal day. The whole of old Ahmedabad is under curfew but that is another distributor area. Even on this side of Sabarmati in our New Ahmedabad area, only seven routes ran out of twenty. What to do sir the shopkeepers are not ready to stock soft drinks because there are hardly any people in the outlets and they are not sure till when will all this last?' he said worriedly.

'Yeah! That is true. I hope this ends soon and our business is back to normal. Has something like this happened earlier Anwar Bhai? You belong to this place so you would know,' I asked him with concern.

He paused for a while, 'No sir never. At-least I have not seen or heard anything like this before. In the same place when there was an earthquake a year back, people from different communities be it Muslim or a Hindu, had made every effort to come out of the calamity, together. I know of so many Hindu families who gave shelter to their distraught Muslim neighbors whose dwellings were swallowed by the earthquake and vice-versa. But I do not know what has happened this time. The same people who were united in a calamity a year back are ready to kill each other today in the name of religion. My heart bleeds when I see this happening to Gujarat, my own state and my home. I live in Kalupur in Old Ahmedabad and I can't tell you how that area is affected. We were staying there till a day back but then it became impossible. Sounds of gun-shots, explosives and religious chants of Hindus and Muslims reverberated throughout the night. My wife is bed ridden with cancer and both my sons are young. They were terrified and could not sleep the whole night. The younger one was burning with fever last night. So I decided to move them today to a relative's house near Vasna, after the police relaxed the curfew for a couple of hours. What to do sir? Cannot let them suffer plus I have a responsibility here in the godown as well. I have to earn a living too. But this riot has changed Gujarat; both the communities are looking at each other differently. I can actually feel the change in the way they look at each other,' he said candidly with eyes full of tears.

Anwar Bhai's understanding of the situation was realistic enough to enable a political novice like me realize the changing societal dynamics in the state. The situation was far worse than a few hundred killings that twenty odd television channels were reporting. The rudimentary soul of the state was bruised and that would perhaps take years to heal.

I was surrounded by my thoughts, in the mean-time Anwar Bhai had moved back to his work. I was disgusted to see the evil faces of route agents Hiren and Jignesh who entered the office. They greeted me informally and walked towards Anwar Bhai.

'Anwar, we are in a hurry. Just take this cash and settle our accounts. We need to leave fast. It is not safe to be out at this time,' Hiren said in a demanding manner.

'Hold your horses Hiren, let me finish with these guys first, then I will settle accounts with you. Even I need to go home and my family is waiting for me too,' he said engrossed in the settlement software on the computer.

'I don't care what you do. You guys are the root cause of this problem in Gujarat. It is because of people like you that we have all these riots and problems. You guys do not believe in us or the country. Just settle our accounts,' Hiren roared.

'What do you mean; I am as much taxed and screwed with all this. The least I want is a lecture from you guys who have been breaking rules right, left and centre. I need to answer Dakshesh Bhai every day on the finances, and you guys take it so lightly. Hang on for a moment before I come to you. And lastly it is not me but some guys in both our communities who are causing all this. I am as much a part of this state and the nation as you are. So please watch your tongue before you speak,' Anwar Bhai said angrily as he looked up at those two goons.

Jignesh sprang into action now, 'Anwar just do your work before we lose it. Just settle us off.'

I walked towards the door and soon their angry voices faded in the background. Times were changing and personal squabbles had taken religious overtones. I went up the stairs; the office looked empty with about thirty percent attendance. DK was busy in his budgetary calculations.

'Hi DK, it's surprising to find you here,' I said. DK lived in the city quite far from the office, hence he was least expected in the office at such a time.

'Oh Hello Boss! I had some work today plus my daughter has her coaching classes in Navrangpura. She has already missed a couple of days so I decided to drop her there in the afternoon and get on with my work. Now I will pick her up in the evening. Yeah it is actually pretty bad in the city. Very scary and painful. I am sure you would be catching the latest through television channels:' I nodded and dropped the idea of going into my cabin.

Bhavna hugged me joyously and kissed me on the cheek as she saw me. I left my bag at the entrance and planted myself on the mattress. She came and lay down next to me with her head on my lap.

I stroked her hair lovingly, 'So how was your trip baby and how do things look at your office?'

'Oh don't ask, the trip was very hectic. I hate such formal occasions but I guess sometimes your presence is mandatory. I am sure my marriage will be as formal and with as many functions,' she said.

'Oh that is painful, I would hate such formality,' I said instantaneously.

She looked at me with an expression of mock disbelief, 'Hullo! Who's talking about your view mister? This is my marriage.'

I was caught red-handed and turned my face towards the balcony.

'Yeah, I meant whoever the poor groom is. He would hate all these functions,' I said.

'No, he won't, he would do whatever I tell him, understand!' she said. "Ok?" I shrugged my shoulders.

'Come close to me,' she whispered. I lifted her inverted face close to me and we kissed deeply.

'I love you Bhavna,' I said and kissed her more.

Intense passion took over our senses and the heart longed for more. It was not possible to be estranged anymore physically. There on that mattress in the living room we made love for the first time. Surrounded with rising hatred and fear in the city, love blossomed in that three bedroom apartment.

14
That Night Stood Still

DK called up early at 8am. Bhavna slept in my arms peacefully and I had no intentions of waking her up.

I got out of the room to take his call, 'Yeah DK what is it?'

'Boss, Good Morning. I hope I did not disturb you. A small issue seems to be cropping up in some markets because of these riots,' he said. "

'What has happened now? As it is we are losing sales day by day,' I said checking out my looks into the room mirror.

'Boss the Baroda distributor called up late last night and said that the retailers are not agreeing to take Uni-Cola promotional stocks and are averse to put up the advertising material of our promotion,' he said.

'But why the hell DK?' I almost howled.

'The shopkeepers are saying that the promotion advertisement on TV has Shahnawaz Khan featuring in it and so does the advertising material like posters. The Hindu outlets are not agreeing to put that up and are threatening to boycott the products that are being endorsed by Muslim actors,' he said animatedly.

It was the stupidest thing that I had ever heard in my life.

'What bull-shit! What has a poor movie star got to do with riots in Gujarat? Tomorrow the same people will say that we do not want a president who is a Muslim. Will we tolerate it?' I yelled again.

'Boss I understand that but what to do, it's not me or the distributors but the market that is reacting in this manner. I don't think boss that it is one of those lame excuses where they are trying to find out another way of not delivering their targets,' he said with some logic in his statement.

I was still not convinced that the situation was all that grave.

'Okay DK, I will try and visit Baroda today for a few hours and put some sense into the distributor. Maybe I will also go and visit a few outlets and test out the market reality myself,' I said.

'Are you sure you would want to do that Boss? It's not the best time for traveling and *Amdavad* will be under curfew after eight,' he asked sounding worried.

'I would be back much before that; I am spending only a couple of hours there. Relax DK, let me go and check this one out,' I said and hung up.

'Good Morning, when did you get up?' Bhavna said as she entered the room.

She looked quite desirable even though she was looking somewhat ruffled and muzzy. 'Nothing yaar, some stupid thing happening all across this place. It is so fucking ridiculous that I don't even find it worthwhile to mention. Seems like I will have to go to Baroda today,' I said hopelessly.

'Oh! Isn't that a bit risky? You do not even have your driver today. Shouldn't you be organizing a cab?' she said, washing her face in the basin next to the kitchen.

'It's ok, too much of a hassle .By the time I do all that and the cab reaches here it will be twelve. I want to leave in next one hour so that

I am back latest by eight in the evening. The entry to Baroda highway is through Vasna and that will be under curfew from 8pm. I want to be back by then,' I said picking up my towel for a shower.

'Ok. Take care. What do you want for breakfast,' she said.

'Bread and eggs would do otherwise whatever you may have,' I shouted from the bathroom and turned on the shower.

When I came out of the wash room, Bhavna was humming, 'Honesty is such a lonely word. Every body is so untrue.'

'Is this your favorite song?' I asked her.

'You know what? I love the lyrics. An honest person is always alone.'

I shrugged as if it was difficult to understand.

I was on my way to Baroda in an hour and it took me less than thirty minutes to reach there than a normal day. The highway presented a similar story and wore the same deserted look. A considerable part of the day was spent with Pradeep Bhai the owner of Surya Distributors listening to his market tales about how a harmless piece of advertising i.e. a poster and a banner, were disrupting the communal harmony of an already butchered state. The solution I offered him was simple, fold the part on the poster and the banner that features that guilty Shahnawaz Khan and then put it up. Pradeep Bhai stated numerous reasons of why that was not possible; the causes ranged from lack of time to non-availability of safety pins for folding the poster. What he could not offer was one single solution for the problem. There seemed no point in arguing with him. I told him to send one stapler with each of the route agent. If the shopkeeper objected, he could just staple the objectionable side. Pradeep Bhai agreed and I heaved a sigh of relief. I knew well that he bought into the idea not because of its ingenuity but also because I agreed that

TUCC would fund the cost of staplers and the pins when his army goes out in the market everyday. This little victory brought some joy into our lives. I went to the market after that but more than half of the shops were shut and the others were waiting for slightest of indications to down their shutters.

By the time I passed the outskirts of Baroda it was already seven thirty by my watch.

'Damn, I should have left an hour back. I hope I get there by curfew time,' I muttered angrily to myself.

My favorite music by Reo Speedwagon played in the car but I was paying more attention to my watch and the speedometer than the melody. It was pitch dark when I passed the TUCC plant. It looked majestic at night as the lights fell on the impressive building placed at some distance from the main gates. There were no trucks in front of the gates, a clear indication of troubled business in the state. As I looked around I was filled with apprehension, the only car on the road was mine. I drove for about five minutes and felt good when I met a group of four trucks driving together on the highway. They were zipping at a good speed because of the empty road and I felt secure with them. A couple of kilometers later they stopped at one of the open small highway *dhabas* on the side of the road, and I was left to fend for myself on the lonely stretch. This was perhaps the only time I was alone on the highway. You get to see a lot of Hollywood movies with empty stretches and highways, but here in India this was a rare treat. Nonetheless I wasn't enjoying it one bit. On a normal day I would crib incessantly about the highway traffic while traveling to the plant and today when there was none I was praying to find a companion. There were hardly any lights on the highway; and most of the restaurants that I passed were shut with one odd eatery open under dim lights. All the fancy glow-signs on the highway were switched off to avoid any unwanted attention. A row of trucks was parked outside a few open eateries, reluctant to progress on their journey at night. I had no such option but to carry further till I reached my safe habitat, into her arms.

It was eight forty five and I was very close to the Vishala Toll, the entry point into the city. The barricade looked lonely and un-guarded. The secluded highway had taken a toll on my bearings and I was glad to see the gateway that provided an access to the society of people. I raced towards the gateway. The barricade was coming closer. A multitude of torches and human forms appeared on the road from nowhere and compelled me to brake. The car screeched a few meters and came to a dead halt.

Around ten policemen armed with a torch and a rifle in each of their hands descended on the car.

'Stop there! Where do you think you are going? Do you want to get killed mister?' one of them yelled at me.

'Oh! What has happened? Actually I need to get into the city soon, I am late and someone in the family is not keeping well,' I faked a reason.

'What?? Have you gone crazy? Forget someone sick at home, your life will be in danger too if you go. Don't you know that this part of the city is under curfew after eight, and there have been fresh incidents of violence in Vasna today? The entry into the city is out of question till six in the morning. You better turn back to Anand or Baroda for the night,' he said sternly.

The other policemen kept staring at me attentively, ready to shoot the lunatic if he didn't listen.

'Please try to understand boss, nothing big will happen if you allow one single person to enter. Where will I go? I am already coming from Baroda. If you want to be sure about my credentials well I am from TUCC and my getting into the city is important. Please let me in,' I tried to plug in the MNC reference hoping that it worked.

'TUCC?? Huh what were you doing so late at night? Selling soft-drinks?' he sneered and looked at his uncouth buddies.

'No sir, I cannot allow you at any cost. Tomorrow something happens to guys like you because of your own stupidity, and we are blamed by the media and our seniors officials that why did we allow this to happen. Why don't you go and spend the night at your own plant, which will be better,' he said and turned back.

The other policemen signaled me to turn back with their rifles indicating that my argument time in their court was over.

'Fuck, fuck, fuck. What do I do now?' I cursed as I turned my car back.

I parked it next to a closed restaurant about a hundred feet from the toll. The only possible solution that seemed to me was requesting those stubborn souls again after some time.

'Sir, do you want to get into the city?' a voice emanating from the left hand window of my car said to me.

I looked sideways and a young guy in police uniform was staring at me. On close supervision I realized that he was one amongst the herd that I had encountered a few minutes back.

'Yeah, I want to but you guys only denied me entry a few minutes back,' I said expectedly.

He opened the door without a hitch and sat next to me, 'Oh that is fine, that is duty! I can take you to the city, not through the toll but from another road that is safe. But it will cost you five hundred rupees,' he said looking at me.

I wanted to get back desperately for sure but paying five hundred rupees as a bribe for driving a couple of kilometers into my own city was a bit too much.

'That is too steep mister! I can't pay that much?' I said looking to bargain.

The guy gave me a desperate look, 'Sir, you know how tough it is to get into the city at this hour and even then you talk like this? You will have to travel back to Baroda on this desolate highway, tell me will that be safe? Here I am ready to take you into the city for five hundred rupees and you find it steep, fine,' he sighed and gestured to move out.

I knew I was stuck and he was the only hope.

'Ok, stop. It's fine. Let's go,' I said.

He smiled and reclined on the seat, 'Go straight into the service road adjacent to highway and take a right before the toll on that non-concrete track.'

The road was bumpy. With thick darkness all around, I could barely see what lay ahead. 'I hope there isn't a pothole or something on the road, I can't see properly,' I told my navigator.

'Don't worry sir. I pass this way every day. Just drive on without any fear,' he said.

I fixed my eyes as hard as I could on the path and tried to keep the vehicle in the middle. 'Take a left turn from here now,' the policeman said like an expert.

We were on a better surface and I could sense that the Vasna main road was not very far from here. There were some modest houses on both sides of the road indicating that we were in a low income area.

'I want to be back home,' I reiterated in my head as I thought of Bhavna once again.

The silence was broken by a sound that seemed like bursting of many fire-crackers. 'Whoa! What was that?' I said.

'Gunshots, someone is having fun,' he said unmoved, his eyes looking ahead.

The gunshots were preceded by religious cries from both communities. It sounded as if two mobs were about to clash.

'What's all that, I hope we are safe?' I said.

'What do you expect to hear at this time sir? People chanting *Bhajans?* Don't worry, we should be fine,' he said coldly amplifying my fear.

He signaled me to stop at the corner.

'I will go from here, you just go straight for two minutes and you will hit the Vasna main road, turn left and after traveling for another five hundred meters take another left and you will get the track to Satellite,' he said and stretched his hand out for money.

'But you had said that you will get me safely into the city and then go, and now you are leaving me in the middle of this empty road?' I retorted.

'What sir? Isn't this the city and haven't I kept my promise? You have to go for another five minutes on a road that is clear. Don't worry nothing will happen to you. I would have come but I need to return to the toll post,' he said hurriedly.

There wasn't any option left but to follow his instructions without wasting any time. I couldn't have argued with him. Reluctantly I took out five hundred rupees from my wallet and handed it over to him. His face shone at the sight of the currency and he got out of the car.

Suddenly he turned back and looked at me, 'Any tip sir?' I nodded in desperation and raced the accelerator. The man was left behind and I saw him retreating in the other direction.

'What a greedy asshole!' I cursed as I took a left on the main road.

It looked completely desolate and quiet. I was getting nervous and could feel the pounding of my heart. I saw a police Gypsy with a loud siren coming towards me on the other side of the road. I slowed down a bit. The policeman driving the gypsy seemed to be puzzled to see a car on the road and then waved frantically at me to get off. I shook my head in affirmation and the Gypsy moved further. I would be a few hundred meters away from the road to Satellite when I saw a mob of hundred appearing on the other side of the road. It was difficult to figure out which community they belonged to but they were brandishing swords and sticks and looked very dangerous. Lunging forward in a group they were ready to kill. My heart sank with fear and I felt it was all over. They had not noticed me till now because I was still some distance away from them on the opposite side. But we were bound to meet soon across each sides of the road divider. I had always read that at times like these when death is impending, your life flashes before you. It was true. I thought of all those closest to me and about Bhavna the most. I was closing on to them, with a dead brain and paralyzed body. I could see them having noticed me and waving their weapons in the air to take action. I pressed the accelerator harder and suddenly my phone rang. It shocked me and somehow I managed to switch it off. The distance was hardly fifty feet and a few of them had crossed over the divider to lunge at my car. I closed my eyes for a moment. Everything stood still and my brain processed the last images seen by my eyes and voices that my ears heard. Scores of angry and ugly faces along with sky shattering noises. Thud, a big sword landed on the bonnet of my car and it zoomed ahead of that brutal mob. I was back in reality. Some of them ran towards the car but gave up the chase after having lost the battle with the machine. I saw them in the rear view mirror looking at me and waving their weapons with resentment. I took a left from the main road and entered a bustling civilization. Never in my life did I feel so good after seeing so many people. My blood pressure came back to normal. I saw the missed call, it was DK.

'Hi boss, how was your trip? Hope you are doing fine,' he said.

I could hear his wife talking in Bengali to his daughter in the background. I laughed at his statement and the irony considering what had actually transpired.

'Yeah just got back. All is fine. Tell me?' I said.

'Boss, I have got a poster sample made for the promotion that does not feature Shahnawaz Khan. I have seen it and it looks fine. If you too like it then I can order about ten thousand of those and get them dispatched by tomorrow night. This will take care of any issue in the market,' he said.

'Oh good, that was fast DK. Where is the sample? I would like to see it ASAP,' I said taking a deep breath.

'It's in the Thaltej office; I have kept it with the guard. Would you be able to see it to-night?' he said hesitatingly.

'Yeah, I will do that. We don't have much time. I will go and take a look at it on my way now,' I said and hung up.

'This should be one of the most eventful nights of my life,' I said to myself and sped towards the Thaltej office.

'Let's just get over with this in the next five minutes and then head towards Bhavna's home straight away,' I said to myself. I took a right from the service road to enter Thaltej office.

Anwar Bhai's face had fear written all over it as it shone in my headlights. I was quick to apply brakes or else the vehicle would have hit him. He now had his hands placed on my bonnet with his body half bent over the car. He looked visibly distraught. A pack of route agents stood behind his thin frame and on the forefront were dangerous looking Hiren and Jignesh.

I peeped out of the car, 'What is the matter guys, what is happening here? Isn't Dakshesh in the go down?'

'Nothing sir, just want to teach this bastard Anwar a little lesson. These guys are a pain to everyone, be it us or to this state or the nation,' Jignesh laughed with disdain.

'You cheat, I am going to report everything to Dakshesh tomorrow morning first thing about all the mess you have created in the market,' Anwar Bhai snapped back.

The group had cornered the poor soul and was up against him. None of the others could stand up to Hiren and Jignesh hence they followed them like meek slaves.

Hiren pushed Anwar Bhai, 'What will you do bloody Anwar? Go and complain to Dakshesh Bhai huh? Go and we will also see how do you do that.'

'Hey guys stop it, this is not the time,' I said hurriedly trying to resolve the matter.

'You please go *sahib* and let us resolve this matter amongst ourselves,' Jignesh said animatedly.

I drove inside the go down and parked the car. I looked back to see both of them pushing and perhaps slapping the poor soul. Anwar Bhai was continuously arguing with them and trying to save himself from their blows. But the small mob carried on in the darkness and soon the voices disappeared. I climbed up the stairs and checked out the sample DK had left with the guard. It was indeed good. I got down the stairs to my car and looked around, the godown was silent and the agents seemed to have left. Perhaps the squabble had got over; I thought as I sat in the car. My headlights flashed over about a dozen broken glass bottles of Uni-Cola lying at the main gate.

'These were not here when I came in. So how come they are here now?' I wondered.

Bhavna opened the main door and hugged me.

'Hey how have you been? I had started getting worried. You did not call the whole day too,' she said.

'Oh! What a day! Don't even ask,' I said and lay down flat on the mattress.

We spent the next one hour talking about perhaps one of the most memorable days of my life. I skipped the incident about Anwar Bhai though.

'You saw it the other day and did not talk about it when you met me. Why Chandan?' her words assaulted me further.

'Because I thought it was a normal scuffle between people working in the same office. I never thought it would go beyond that,' I said.

'But why were you hiding it for god's sake from me for so many days

even after knowing everything. If I wouldn't have got to know it by myself you would have always kept it hidden?' she shouted again.

'Do you know Chandan, you acted like a spineless wimp? Just like Arjun!' she said.

15
The Big Deceit

Yesterday's experience was quite exhausting to my body and mind. It kept me in bed till about nine thirty in the morning.

B2 called up, 'Hello Boss! Good morning. Will you be coming to the office today? I wanted to discuss the agreement of City Hall Multiplex that is up for renewal. This guy is asking for a thirty percent increase over his last agreement.'

I replied drowsily, 'B2, I will see you in the office in an hour or so, let us talk then,' I said.

Bhavna had left early for work and the house seemed empty without her. I recalled that I had dozed off last night without any dinner. I entered the kitchen and the sight of appetizing Maggi noodles and half fried eggs in the microwave thrilled me.

'What a bloody killer product? Maggi noodles, it has changed the way India snacks and an absolute life saver for single guys like us,' I muttered and dug into the maze of tasty noodles thanking Bhavna for the snack.

I noticed a blue police gypsy parked in front of the city office. A scary thought crossed my mind.

'I hope the police van did not note my car number when I was speeding in the curfew zone last night. Arrey, but how can they come here so fast Chandan? Even if they have the number it will take them at least a couple of days to scan through all car registration numbers. Not possible. Relax!' I comforted myself.

I climbed up the stairs and glanced around. The attendance seemed better today. Almost a week had passed since the riots had erupted but normalcy seemed far off. B2 was engrossed on his computer, checking his pending mails that had accumulated over the last few days.

'Boss did you get to know about Anwar Bhai?' DK entered my room suddenly.

My heartbeat amplified two hundred times and my voice trembled, sensing something unexpected, 'No! What happened to him?'

DK pushed himself onto the chair and replied coldly, 'It seems that he was murdered last night while he was on his way back home from the office. His body was found in butchered state about five hundred meters from our office, in the barren field behind. Must be these fanatics, who else?' I could feel my heart sinking.

'Did I expect something like this even in my wildest imagination? No not at all! Should I talk about it now, that I was a witness to this? Should I wait?' thoughts fluttered all across my clogged mind.

'The cops are here and they have spoken to Dakshesh and other route agents, but none of them have anything worthwhile to report. All they had to say was that after the day's work all of them returned home. They had no clue as to how Anwar Bhai reached there?' DK's words cut through the uncanny silence in my cabin.

'What piece of bull shit? All those goons were bloody fighting with poor Anwar and those bastards Hiren and Jignesh were in the fore-front, and they are not ready to acknowledge that! I saw it. Should I say it here? Not now I guess, a thousand rumors will float. Let me think this through of how to take it forward. This is not the platform,' I thought as I looked at DK without letting any emotion show on my face.

I reclined on the chair and closed my eyes.Anwar Bhai's helpless face kept gazing at me for a long time.

I could not do a thing the entire day. It was about five in the evening when I walked into Dakshesh's office. The office was desolate and Anwar's empty seat with the portraits of different Hindu deities on the wall behind lay speechless. Dakshesh was alone and busy playing his game on the computer.

'How are you *sahib*? Have you seen the condition of our Gujarat? It's going to the dogs. The market has been completely down for so many days. This month's sale is gone sir. I am going to suffer huge losses,' the fat bugger said in a concerned voice, his eyes fixed on the computer screen.

'All bloody bullshit, the ass is the least concerned,' I thought.

'Why didn't your agents tell you that they had a fight with Anwar Bhai last night? And they were very much with him till about 10pm?' I asked him sternly.

Dakshesh looked up, 'Array Sahib what is the big deal? I know about it. These fights between people working together are common every where, and this office is no exception. These guys had told me in the morning but there was no point in talking about it in front of the police. Unnecessarily they would have asked a thousand questions. So many complications. Who wants to get into them? I only told my guys to feign ignorance. It is a bad time *sahib*; one man is killing the other one. Poor Anwar, I am sorry about him. But who can challenge destiny, the man had to go.'

I reacted irately, 'But your men were blinded with fury. I was a witness to it myself. I really do not know what happened last night…'

I was cut short by Dakshesh, 'Nothing happened sir. It was a small argument that ended abruptly. When Anwar was returning home, he was confronted by a religious mob and they murdered him after finding out his identity. The time is bad sir, what to do? The police have also come to a similar conclusion" he said and focused his gaze on the screen again.'

'Yeah Dakshesh, just because the riots are in vogue these days it does not mean that everyone who is conking off is dying in them. There are natural deaths, murders and calamities too so let us not assume that he would have died in riots,' I said.

'So what do you think sir, how did he die if the mob did not kill him?' Dakshesh said looking into my eyes.

I wanted to tell him that I believed that his own faithful scoundrels Jignesh and Hiren killed the helpless guy and none of his other agents could stand up and save him. But the words did not leave my throat.

'Well I do not know Dakshesh but at least your guys could have spoken the truth,' was my feeble reply.

'No point sir it wouldn't have achieved anything except complications with the law,' he said.

I stood there for a couple of minutes looking at the inconsiderate guy who felt zero pain at the loss of Anwar Bhai. I turned back and walked towards the door.

'But sir these guys have played dirty too. They started all this bloody tension in this state and now one amongst them had to pay a steep price for it. So what to do? And who is to be blamed?' Dakshesh said bitterly. I looked back at him in disgust and walked out.

'So how are things at the office? Is your sales back on track again or are you guys going to get fired by your American bosses this year?' Bhavna said while opening the pizza box from Upper Crust.

I sat motionless on the living room mattress.

I smiled feebly, 'What sales? We are badly fucked Bhavna. It's not just going to end with this season but will impact our business plans for the whole year.'

'Oh my baby! Don't make this face. I am sure everyone around the globe is tuned to the ruckus that has afflicted Gujarat. I am sure they would understand,' she said sounding concerned.

'Hmmm....they will understand till the time it does not affect their performance and price of the stocks at Wall Street. If it does then no one will understand. All these so called multi-nationals function like this,' I said.

She didn't look very convinced with my generalization but still nodded.

'What about you Bhavna? You seem to be working hard too,' I said.

'Array, this is party time for a news channel like ours. It's too much work and very little time. It is better this time because I have a couple of people from Mumbai to help me out at work otherwise it is crazy,' she said moving around a largish piece of pizza in her mouth.

'Would you like to eat something?' she said.

'No I am fine; I guess I will sleep now. Are you going early tomorrow?' I said getting up. 'No I will leave around ten. But why are you sleeping so early baby? Wait for some time please?' she held my hand and looked deep into my eyes. Her eyes flickered with naughtiness.

'I am really tired baby and I want to get early into the office. Before that I want to peek into my flat as well. Just want to go there once, haven't been there for ages now,' I said.

My plans of getting up early went for a toss as I slept till late. DK's phone call woke me up.

'Boss are you coming over to the office?' he sounded concerned.

'Yeah, I will. What's the matter? Anything urgent?' I asked in a sleepy voice

'Nothing very critical Boss. Anwar Bhai's wife and kids are here, they want to meet someone senior from the company. Since you are the senior most in this office I thought they should be meeting you,' he said sounding a bit unnerved.

Sleep disappeared from my eyes.

'Isn't Dakshesh there? Shouldn't he be meeting them too? What is she saying?' I said. 'He does not want to, has been avoiding them. She wants to talk to a senior company official sir. I thought it would be good if you could meet them once,' DK pressed again. '*Is it about Anwar's murder*? Has she come to know from someone that I had met Anwar that night? Does she want to meet me because of that?' I blurted out unconsciously. There was silence on the line. I guess I spoke the unspeakable.

'Did you sir? Well I did not know that. What did he say? Do you know what happened with him?' DK bombarded a flurry of questions.

'Well nothing much. I just saw him in the godown when I came into office late that night. Nothing else DK. This is sensitive DK. I hope you will keep it to yourself,' I said hoping to end this topic.

'I will be in office in a while, but not so early. It would be better that I meet up with his family later,' I ended the conversation and disconnected the call.

'Do you have the balls to face them Chandan?' my inner voice shrieked within as I turned back. She was standing there. Her eyes staring at me.

'Why did you lie to me?' she said.

Her expression changed and I could see tears trickling freely down her cheeks.

'What Bhavna? I did not lie to you. It was just one small incident on that bloody horrendous day. I did not even remember it in the whole scheme of things. I forgot about it, so what's the big deal?' I shrugged.

I took a step towards the door. She was blocking my way and by no chance could I escape her questions. I stood still.

'What do you want me to tell you Bhavna? Ok I met Anwar Bhai that night and he was involved in some stupid brawl with the depot route agents. I tried to sort out their altercation but it was an internal issue and I could not help beyond a point. So I left it there, finished my work and came back home. I was so goddamn exhausted both physically and mentally that I did not have the energy to pursue the matter further,' I said hoping that this would cool her down a bit.

The tears had found another ground on her face and were running furiously on the cheeks.

'So, did you have inkling that something would have happened to Anwar or no?' she said in a voice choked with tears.

'Well I had, but I do not know whether his death is a result of that fight or he was caught unaware by a fanatic mob,' I said.

'Stop lying any further please, I beg of you,' she shouted as she broke down.

'You saw it the other day and did not talk about it when you met me. Why Chandan?' her words assaulted me further.

'Because I thought it was a normal scuffle between people working in the same office. I never thought it would go beyond that,' I said.

'But why were you hiding it for god's sake from me for so many days even after knowing everything. If I wouldn't have got to know it by myself you would have always kept it hidden?' she shouted again.

'Do you know Chandan, you acted like a spineless wimp? Just like Arjun!' she said.

Her words hurt me like an inferno and I lost control. A comparison with Arjun was the last straw.

'What the hell do you mean Bhavna? I did not lie to you purposely. I am sorry about Anwar Bhai but what about me? Don't you love me? Am I not as close to you as your Anwar Bhai?' I said theatrically.

'No one is closer to me than my belief and values. You have really hurt me very deeply today. I never expected that someone whom I love so dearly would let me down so badly. It's not about the death of Anwar Bhai. I can live with it. It's about you acting weakly, hiding things that could have perhaps helped in discovering the truth behind his murder. I have nothing more to say to you and I would appreciate if you leave my house and my life right now,' she said sternly.

It felt as if a thousand hard slaps had landed on my face together. Anger, hurt and disbelief crippled me and I walked into the other room to pick my suitcase up. In a few minutes I was at her door with my bag.

'Bhavna, maybe we can talk about it calmly. I am sorry if I have hurt you but I think you are acting hastily. It's too severe an action for what I have done,' I said standing at the door.

'Yes I am a witness to it but you cannot push me to feel the same pain as his family. We are different individuals leading different lives, facing

different circumstances and having different problems,' I said mixing contorted logic with philosophy.

'But we are humans who are bonded together with a string of compassion. There is no point in being compassionate and not having courage to stand up for what is right. Compassion by itself is pointless. No point in feeling bad for the poor one legged beggar knocking on your car window wearing tattered clothes. Everyone does it. If you have the balls, get out of the car and help him, mind you not just by giving him money. But help him by making his life better from that moment is what I call compassion backed by courage. Do you have it in you Chandan?' she said looking at me. I was scared.

She kept sitting on the chair looking towards the window.

'Please leave me alone and never try to meet me,' she said. I looked at her and walked out of the house.

It was quite hot outside and I was perspiring by the time I reached the parking lot. I looked up hoping against odds to find her in the balcony. The balcony was vacant. The feeling of losing her was not ready to precipitate.

Was it over?

16
Love Bleeds

The empty two bedroom apartment welcomed its dweller with open arms. The dimly lit rooms seemed happy to brighten up with warm sunshine as I brushed the dark curtains aside and opened the windows. A long stay with Bhavna had added a sense of unfamiliarity with my own abode and I felt a bit of a stranger out here. Uncertain times in the state and an equally tentative relationship status was enough to sap me of my energies making me absolutely averse of going for work. I lay down on the sofa in my living room and looked at the pale ceiling. Soon slumber engulfed my emotionless body.

I woke up pretty numb at about 2 pm. I got ready for work mechanically and reached the office. The work place appeared more normal than before. The office had almost eighty percent attendance and being lunch hour the staff was busy filling each other with stories from the riots. Each one of them had a story more gruesome than the other and their narration was peppered with details that made everyone re-live those dark moments again. DK was in the middle of one such story and listened to the gory tales of human brutality. Pretty un-noticed I passed the chatty pack, entered my cabin and got immersed in the multitude of e-mails that were ensconced in my inbox.

Sumo called at 5 when I was in middle of the web world, 'What the hell is happening at Thaltej?' he asked all keyed up.

My numb tranquility was abruptly shaken by his alarmed tone, 'What is the matter Sumo? Anything wrong?'

'The Thaltej office is swarmed with media guys from the Newsplus channel. They are hounding Dakshesh with all kinds of questions regarding death of his office accountant.

He has called me about twenty times in the last twenty minutes asking me to do something. Don't you know this?' he said.

'No Sumo, I don't,' I said, thinking all alongthat this was cent percent Bhavna's doing.

It couldn't be anyone else but her, who could take so much of an interest in the uncanny death of a measly accountant. It was her speed this time that amazed me more than her strong will.

'So what do you want me to do Sumo? Let Dakshesh give the same statement to the media that he is giving to everyone,' I said.

'No, not at all Chandan, we cannot let that happen. Media is going to cover this story in a very different manner; they are going to talk about the mysterious death of an accountant working with an MNC and not with a distributor. We may get bad press all over and that is something we cannot afford at this juncture. We cannot afford bad publicity on top of a shortfall in sales. We may get clobbered. This should not happen,' he almost cried out.

I just did not know what was playing in Sumo's mind. How could I prevent the media from talking to Dakshesh?

'You must do something. You guys interact with media, put so much of money in advertising, you people can put pressure on these media guys not to harass a poor distributor. Tell them we will come out with an official statement but let us not create a *hangama* in the office,' he said.

'Sumo, I can't do that. Why will they listen to me? Editorial anywhere is independent of advertising. They can probe or cover anything they wish to. I do not think it is possible?' I almost pleaded.

'Just go and try Chandan, I am sure you guys can do it. Put pressure on them; just get them away at this hour. Oh shit! This guy Dakshesh is calling again, I am telling him that you will try and do something to get them off his back now. Ok?' Sumo said a bit firmly. 'But Sumo…why are we supporting this guy so much, let's face it, he is a distributor and not a part of the company. I mean why should we be saving him when we ourselves are not sure of the truth. Who knows how that accountant died?' I said.

'I am not too interested in the discovery of truth now Chandan. We are here trying to salvage a hopeless situation where media may put up a bad story on Unicola Company, which is completely avoidable at this time. Please go and try to stop that rather than arguing with me on the phone,' he replied sternly.

I nodded in desperation, 'Ok boss, I will try and do my best.'

I pulled the curtain of my window and could see the News Plus Outdoor Broadcast van standing in front of the godown gate. I got out of the room swiftly and asked DK to follow me.

Bhavna was downstairs, standing in front of the closed door of Dakshesh's office with her crew, waiting.

'Hey, hi there! What are you guys upto? I am told that you want the distributor to come out and give you a statement. Well, what is the impending hurry? The guy is not feeling too well today, and we will issue a release that answers all your questions,' I said rigidly. 'Mr. Mathur, we are not here to create any trouble for your distributor. A man has died under mysterious circumstances and he happens to be the employee of your distributor. We are here to know more about the context and we want your distributor to answer some of our questions, that's it,' she replied with equal firmness.

'Have you guys taken on the responsibility of local police? He has already given his statement to the police and they are on the job. Why are you guys unnecessarily creating a scene here? You are harming the reputation of my company. I would really request you to leave from here right now,' I said.

'Isn't that reputation already under a scanner? An employee dies in your distributor's office and it is dismissed as a death caused by riots. I want to get complete details about that night. I am told there were a whole lot of people here and I would like to meet all of them along with a statement from you, if you are the senior-most employee here Mr. Mathur,' she said.

DK looked completely perplexed with the strange familiarity in our verbal duel. People from the office and the route agents had started crowding around us and I could sense the tension building up.

'No way Bhavna, you guys just can't do what you want and when you want. Dakshesh is not going to speak to you right now. If you guys do not leave our premises I will be forced to call my lawyers and inform the police. We are a law abiding company and we are entitled to our freedom,' I said while pulling out the mobile phone from my pocket. One of her colleagues whispered something in Bhavna's ears for a few seconds.

Her face had disgust written all over as she looked at me, 'Ok, we are going now but do not think that this is over. We are not going to let go of an innocent life so easily till we have dug out the complete truth. I request you Mr. Mathur that some of you who may know about it should come out in the open and talk to us like men,' Bhavna turned back abruptly and walked towards the gate.

My spirit seemed to be walking away from my body and I could do nothing to retrieve it. I felt as if the universe was conniving to separate me from Bhavna at any cost.

Five minutes after they had left, Dakshesh came out with a sheepish smile on his face. 'Thank you *sahib,* I was telling Sumo sir that we do so much for the company so at difficult times the company should also step forward to protect us,' he said.

I looked at the snake in disdain, the one I had protected, and hurt my love terribly again in the bargain.

My phone beeped as I was driving out of the office. It was a message from Bhavna, 'You lied. I really do not care much about you turning me out of the office today. I am more disgusted with your attitude of not believing in what is right. I cannot take that and I do not want to meet you. Ever.'

I flipped through various channels on the television till about eight thirty impassively. The mind kept playing images of Bhavna repeatedly in different *avatars* that hurt each time they appeared. Like any other troubled soul on the planet, I reached for my bottle of whiskey and poured myself a stiff drink and gulped it in five minutes. I had three more of them and by the time I got up I was already high.

It was close to twelve when I reached Bhavna's apartments. I was in two minds about barging into her house at this hour but frankly I had no other alternative. It was better to meet her at that hour than going crazy. The guard at the building gate let me go in without any telephonic audit with Bhavna purely because of the familiarity that we had developed during my brief stay at her place. I looked up the high rise; the building was a perfect example of the cosmopolitan culture seeping up in the city that also brushed sides with deep rooted Guajarati sentiments. It gave shelter to a real live in relationship right here in the so called traditional Ahmedabad. That relationship seemed to be in doldrums and I wanted to sort that out.

I could hear no sound for a minute after I rang her doorbell. I looked at the watch and my imperfect demeanor. 'I shouldn't be here at this hour and in this state. But what to do, I can't survive either, if I do not meet her?' I played this question and answer battle in my mind as I pressed the doorbell again. After a few seconds I could hear her footsteps approaching the door. I straightened a bit trying to hold myself better.

Bhavna opened the door and looked at me as if she was expecting me,'So why are you here? I have told you that I do not have anything for you now. Why do you keep coming back to me again and again when it's all over? How the hell can I make you understand this dammit?' she almost yelled.

'But Bhavna listen to me please for once. You may be right but I owe you an explanation too. Give me that chance Bhavna, if I am here at this hour it means that it's killing me from inside and that I really love you and I do not want to lose you. Please let me come in and explain,' I almost pleaded in a hushed tone.

'No not at all Chandan. I have nothing to say to a man who fucking lies to someone he loves. I have seen enough and I have no intentions of taking this any further and getting hurt any more. Got it? Just go! It's not the right time to talk as people sleep early in Ahmedabad and an inebriated man outside a single girl's door would not be the best of sights for anyone,' she said as she started pulling back the door to lock it.

I looked at her with a mixed feeling of anger and helplessness and then pushed the door to enter her house.

'What do you mean Bhavna? Is it only you who decides about our relationship when both of us are in it together? I have told you repeatedly that I did not tell you about Anwar Bhai because I was not sure and I did not want to upset you further. I am still not too sure whether it is a cold blooded murder or a riot killing,'

'So what am I supposed to do, go out on streets and shout justice for him? Or come to your channel and give a statement about who killed him? What should I do god dammit when I am not too sure about the truth myself?' I reacted emotionally.

Bhavna latched the door and sat on one of the chairs.

I was resting my back against the living room wall and sitting on the mattress.

'You don't love me Chandan,' she said.

'Why? Who says so? Just because I have not told you this one thing that you expected me to tell you does not mean that I do not love you,' I argued with her.

'Knowing fully well that this was the only thing that I expected from you in our relationship, if you could not keep just this one promise of being truthful then you certainly don't love me. Why did you hurt me again Chandan? Why, after Arjun, you too did the same thing! Why??' she screamed and then started sobbing.

I was sitting on the same mattress where we had made love for the first time. I could not gather myself to get up and stop her from crying. I just sat there speechless.

Both of us kept looking at each other for a few minutes in silence.

Bhavna seemed to be in a quandary and she finally spoke, 'But have you at least been able to speak to anyone about what you saw? Today you were not even ready to let go of a simple statement from your distributor.' I kept looking at her.

'Bhavna you guys were in my office premises. Do you know how media shy these MNC's are? My boss was so worried about media landing up at our office. He was fucking on my head. I had no other alternative but to drive you guys out by hook or by crook,' I pleaded. More silence prevailed and neither of us moved from our places.

'But you are pretty sure that those two guys did it. Aren't you?' she said breaking the silence.

'Yeah, I am. Well yes!'

'So will you speak up the truth about what you saw, in your company and to the police and media?' she questioned me.

'I will if the need arises. But it will be my version, and it may not be hundred percent true,' I said.

'So you try and find that out through other agents working for your distributor. Will you do that please? It will be big favor to me, Anwar's family and to justice,' she said.

I nodded in agreement.

'Anwar's family is completely down and out. I met them today in the morning; they are down in the dumps because he was the only earning member. They are low on savings because of his ailing wife and now after his death their situation has worsened. Your bloody distributor has denied anything beyond this month's salary to his widow. It's tough to get anything lawfully too because the cause of his death is uncertain,' she said.

I nodded again, 'I will try and do whatever I can.

After a few minutes Bhavna got up and came closer to me. She leaned on me and kissed me on the lips. I thought we were making love after ages.

17
Agree To Disagree

Next day morning was much better. I was contented to watch Bhavna sleeping in my arms with a child like expression. I stroked her hair gently and she opened her eyes a bit and smiled. I kissed her on the cheeks and hugged her tightly. 'I will never let you go Bhavna,' I said and she dug herself deep into my naked chest. We kept lying like that till 8.30. Finally she got up with an unpleasant expression on her face, unhappy to have got up, and pushed me out of bed as well. We walked out into the living room together.

I was on the sports section of "The Times of India" reading about Tendulkar's shoulder injury when she said to me, 'I want to do a full feature on Anwar Bhai's story. I have the full concept in mind.'

'Hmmm,' I replied not feeling too enthusiastic about shifting my attention from Tendulkar's fitness state to the death of an accountant.

'No actually I want to do a full story on Gujarat riots about how it has become a vent to accomplish personal animosity. Lot of personal enmity is getting resolved by giving it the religious color. I want to cover Anwar Bhai's episode there and maybe you can be featured in that story as well. A witness to the mob fury,' she said engrossed in her thoughts.

'Me! Being covered on TV on this subject? How does that make sense?' I retorted. 'Come on Chandan you said last night that you will say what you saw,' she almost rebuked.

'I am not denying what I said Bhavna, but it needs to have a context and a base. How can my version prove that people are settling personal scores under the garb of riots?' I cried out.

'I am not saying that your version will be presented as conclusive evidence of some kind?' she said and looked up.

'Well yes! You are right for a change. Maybe I should turn the story around a bit,' she suddenly calmed down.

Having won the argument for once with her, I dived back into the world of Tendulkar and cricket.

'Let me do a story around riots disrupting peace and business in the state and you can speak about the adverse effect on the soft-drink business. We will also ask you about the death of your accountant under mysterious circumstances and you can just narrate what you saw, that's it. At-least this will give some relevance to the issue; media will be active on this story and push police to investigate the case better. Ok?' she looked at me.

I looked back into her eyes.

'But what will this achieve Bhavna, I mean Anwar's story would be so much out of context,' I said shrugging.

'It will not be, I will ensure that editorially it is fed well into the main story. Trust me; we will take care of our content. You just speak the truth,' she said.

'But I do not think so; it would sound completely out of place and not look good. I do not think it's a good idea?' I said.

'Why don't you understand that if we do not talk about this unnatural death now, the story is gone? Only if there is media buzz around it, will the administration and police take greater interest in uncovering the truth. I do not understand why are you interested in shoving the truth under the carpet and not talk about it?' she pleaded.

I retreated, 'No Bhavna, I will talk about it. Let me speak internally in the office as well. We need to take prior approvals before speaking to media. You know!'

'Yeah, I know that, but there is nothing official about what you saw. It's the truth and you need to speak that. Speak to your boss, nevertheless. But please do that today, I want to do this story in next two days otherwise it would lose topicality. I will take permission internally and line up all the things by day after. Cool sweetie?' Bhavna looked into my eyes and I nodded in confusion.

I stopped at my apartment on my way to office to take a shower and get into a fresh set of clothes. My life seemed to have improved over the last twelve hours and I felt good getting into the office. The soft drink trucks were on their way to the market as usual. 'How is sales over last two three days?' I asked Sunil the route agent who serviced Vastrapur, where I lived.

Sunil was known to me because he had delivered cases of mineral water at my house while I was down with gastroenteritis a few weeks back.

'Improved very marginally sahib. How much can we push it? People are still not venturing out on the roads,' he replied planted on his seat in Tata 407.

'Okay why don't you wait for five minutes, I will be back after keeping my bag in the cabin. I want to go out in the market for a couple of hours,' I said looking up to him

B2 was working on a client proposal in the office oblivious to the world. I dropped my bag at the reception and climbed down the stairs hurriedly. I jumped into the front seat of the route truck and signaled Sunil to move. The next three hours passed pretty fast in grappling with a market that had lost its buoyancy and was in uncertainty and depression. We walked towards a small eatery in front of the lake at Bodakdev for lunch. Sunil gave some money to his loaders for having lunch.

'The market does not seem to be getting back. It's going to be fucking tough,' desperate words escaped my mouth.

Sunil reciprocated my statement with a confirming look. We sat around an empty table in the restaurant and ordered two Gujarati Thalis. The restaurant décor was absolutely basic and I could see Sunil a bit hesitant in bringing me here. Only a few tables were occupied with company salesmen and some college kids.

'So how is it going Sunil? Hope things are fine in the family,' I asked him while looking for any text messages on my cell phone.

'Yes sahib, things are fine. Luckily I live in a Hindu colony close to the office where it is comparatively safe,' he said.

Sunil then took off with a couple of riot incidents that he knew about, detailing each nuance as if he was personally present there. The entire state of Gujarat like Sunil was talking the riot language. I posed as if I was attentively tuned on to his story while my mind was thinking about the fresh challenges in my life that Bhavna had posed. To come out in the open and talk about what I has seen that night. I believed in what she said but wasn't that too big a risk? Testifying for something that "might" would have happened!

The Gujarati Thali landed on my table and I was back to reality. Sunil was showing no signs of ending his story. My phone beeped in the middle. It was Bhavna.

'Hi how are you doing? Have you reached office?' I said. I hoped against hope that she did not talk about him again.

'Yeah long back. Where are you? Did you get a chance to speak to your boss about the story? I am keeping everything ready for day-after. My boss has agreed to give this story a prime time slot. We have started zeroing in on the panelists; they are going to be Kanta Dave the noted social worker, Bhaskar Das the historian, Sudhanshu Deb the famous lyricist cum writer and you. Lokesh Kohli the star correspondent from News Plus will anchor it and yes I will produce the show. I am so happy Chandan, I am sure that Anwar's murder will get enough relevance for all investigations to happen fast. So have you spoken internally?' she asked in a voice trembling with excitement and happiness.

I went numb again and did not know what to say.

'Great that sounds good Bhavna. Well Sumo has been unreachable since morning, but I will do this by evening. Is it very important to talk about Anwar? Can't I talk about the loss to our businesses in Gujarat at these times?' I said.

'Of course not! You have to talk about your version of what you saw that night. I am doing all this to showcase how a murder can be brushed aside as a death in riots during these times,' she said and hung up. Sunil seemed involved in our conversation. In his late thirties Sunil looked younger than his age. Short in stature he looked athletic.

'Good local food. Have you been here before?' I asked biting a piece of Gujarati roti. He nodded.

'You were also a witness to that dirty fight that night. Isn't it Mathur Sahib?' he continued eating.

I looked at him trying to size up his intentions.

'Yeah, I was, but left it midway. I was in a hurry to leave that night. Why do you ask this?' I inquired.

'I was in that crowd surrounding Anwar when he fell down on the bonnet of your car and you had come out,' he said.

There was silence between us for some time. It was warm inside the restaurant and the two ceiling fans were doing hardly anything to soothe the atmosphere.

'Why didn't you stop the fight sir? Why didn't you order Hiren and Jignesh to spare poor Anwar?' he sounded disturbed as he spoke.

I was motionless for a while and I found it difficult to swallow the portion of food that was in my mouth.

'What would I have done Sunil? I had no idea of what was happening or that it was so serious. I thought it was a matter between you guys to sort out. But no one is sure as well about what happened later. Everyone believes that Anwar was caught by an angry mob and killed. How could I have prevented that?' I said excitedly.

The volume of my voice attracted attention from people sitting around and a couple of them turned to give uncomfortable glances. I tried comforting my swelling excitement. Sunil scorned at me, 'What *sahib* do you think the godown is in a riot infested area? This is one of the safest areas in Ahmedabad where not even a stone pelting incident took place, forget riots and killings. This is all a bloody excuse that Dakshesh and everyone else are handing out to the police. Everyone knows the truth but no one is fucking coming out in the open.'

My head was throbbing by now with multiple images of a pleading Anwar Bhai, the two scoundrels and Bhavna moving at a lightning speed in front of my eyes like a bioscope movie.

I heard myself speaking, 'How do you know that it is a murder and not a riot killing? How are you so sure?'

'Everyone in the company knows that it's Hiren and Jignesh. After that scuffle at the go down gate, a few of us left thinking that it was all over. But I guess it was far from it. The torture continued for quite some time and eventually ended in Anwar's murder. Everyone knows it but no one will come out to speak the truth. All of us are fucking scared of those goons and the distributor. I do not blame us; we are poor people with inaudible and scared voices. We have left our families in villages to come here and earn five thousand rupees. Bloody measly five thousand bucks that just about takes care of our families and children's education. Five thousand rupees that gives us a hope that tomorrow may be better, so just work hard with your heads down and eyes shut. Just keep on going.'

Sunil did not finish his Thali and pushed it away, perhaps with disgust and helplessness that danced wildly on his naïve face. I saw its reflection on my face as well and that amplified my discomfort. The place was suffocating me and so was the conversation. 'Should we go now if we are done Sunil?' I signaled the teenage boy waiter for the bill. 'If you had stopped that fight, Anwar could have been saved sir. I seriously think so,' he repeated again perhaps as an afterthought.

'But even you guys could have done something Sunil? Don't you think so? He was one amongst you and you guys outnumbered those two,' I said seething with anger now. 'Yeah, you are right sahib. Perhaps we could,' he said getting up.

'All of us have played a role in Anwar's death sahib, we all have to answer him, up there,' he said pointing his first finger towards the sky.

I carried an expressionless face outside the restaurant. It was humid and the loaders had returned to the truck. Sunil climbed into the truck and gestured me to hop in.

'I would rather go back Sunil. I have work in the office to finish, I shouted and walked towards a waiting auto rickshaw.

Two convicts charged with a murder pursued different paths that afternoon.

I drove inside the TUCC plant at 5 pm. I was overcome with nervousness and needed someone to stretch out a helping hand. I wished profusely if it could be Sumo.

'So what brings you here Chandan? I received your SMS a while back. Was it that urgent for you to drive all the way down here? We could have talked on phone,' he said going around on his revolving chair.

'It's fine Sumo. I needed to talk about a couple of things and also get these contracts signed. These are high value deals and I am sure you would want clarifications. I thought it is best to get this done personally,' I said as I sat down and placed the contracts on his coffee colored table.

We got through the contracts in half an hour post which I broached the topic of the television interview. Sumo looked at the sky as if an answer would drop from there. Anxiety was gripping my body and the silence was not helping it a bit.

'But why does the same channel that storms into your office one day looking for a scoop , would want to do an interview with you a couple of days later?' he asked looking at my nervous face.

Sumo's eyes were traveling across the topography of my face searching for the right reason. I could sense myself getting interrogated.

'Sumo, there is no issue with News Plus. They had got hold of some news about Anwar's death and they wanted more dope on their story. I pushed them away yesterday saying that TUCC will come out with its version and now they have come back saying that they want to do a full story on Gujarat riots where under the business section they want to cover us. How these riots have thrown business out of gear in a prosperous state such as Gujarat? That's it,' I replied almost in one breath.

'That's what worries me. These journalists I am telling you Chandan, have ulterior motives. It's not as simple as it sounds,' he replied as if he had been a journalist all his life.

'Do not worry Sumo. I will get their questions beforehand. I will be careful,' I said.

Sumo looked apprehensive and I wanted to put things in black and white. 'One more thing Sumo, they know that I was there at the godown the night when Anwar was murdered. They might ask me something about that as well,' I said looking at Sumo. His face was changing color.

He got up from his chair, 'What? You never told me about this. What's all this coming out now? Please give me full details.'

I tried to appear as composed as I could and recounted that night to him verbatim. He seemed to be lost in it for a full five minutes after I had ended the tale.

'So what do you think happened?' he asked me.

'I think he was murdered Sumo and not killed in a riot,' I said.

'How can you be so sure Chandan, you did not see it happening?' he said.I shook my head.

'But everyone knows that he was murdered. I have heard it being talked about all around in the city office Sumo,' I said. I have lived with it for last so many days, so how can you pass a verdict in half an hour Mr. Sumo Sen.

'But all these fellows might have vested interests in implicating those two agents and they haven't been a witness to this "so called" murder either. So how does one believe it and how is it valid in the court of law?' he said in an animated voice.

I reiterated all the valid reasons for the next half hour of how it was a murder but still he did not seem fully convinced.

'I appreciate your honesty and spirit but I am not fully persuaded. Not even one single person has come out as a witness to this murder and on top of it your own distributor is certain that this is a riot killing. So I do not think that you should talk about it to media. It's a half baked truth and may cause more harm to TUCC reputation than good,' he said tossing the contracts towards me. I was going to lose the battle with my manager.

'But Sumo, I am just stating what I saw that night. I am not going to pass a judgment on Anwar's death. Don't you think we owe this truth to the society if not anybody else?' I took my last chance.

'Who pays our salaries Chandan? The society or TUCC? I am as much for truth and justice but not at the sake of harming the organization by speaking half baked truths to media that may spiral to some bigger controversy. I would rather stay away from it. So let's not speak about it,' he said and got up.

I walked to the car parking in silence. The bus carrying the workers for the night shift drove into the plant and I could hear them chatting loudly and singing songs as it drove past me towards the main building. I wish I could tell Sumo that I agreed with my soul mate that it was our job to become the voice that upholds truth. It was our job as well to be the first one to stand up against injustice. It was my job to be the one. But nothing like that happened and what came out of the TUCC plant that evening was a weak human who would attempt to try and uphold his selfish love.

18
Flop Debut On TV

I switched on the home theatre in my living room and tuned it to a private FM station. It was past 9pm and the house was stuffy. I kept the door that connected my living room with the balcony open. I came out in the open and inhaled some fresh air. I wanted to be there for a while. The city was mapped into habitats of different sizes and shapes that looked pleasing at night in the artificial light. I ran down the day in my mind and it looked far from satisfying. An uncomfortable encounter with Sunil, an unfulfilled promise made to Bhavna and a non productive meeting with Sumo. Nothing seemed to be working in my favor. My mobile phone rang inside and I knew it was her. Perplexed and equally nervous, I did not pick it up.

She called again and this time there was no escape. I paused after picking the call, giving her levy to speak first.

'Hey, where have you been? I hope you spoke to Sumo about the interview?' she inquired.

'Yeah, kind of. We had a few other important issues to discuss as well. But yes I talked about it, I don't think it's going to be an issue Bhavna,' I lied while swiping away fresh sweat that had emerged on my forehead.

'Great then. We are all ready for day after. All the panelists have confirmed. I am sure it's going to go well,' she said excitedly. I was silent.

'And I hope Anwar Bhai gets the justice that is due to him,' she said softly as an afterthought.

The trust that she had in me made me uncomfortable. I was not the strong one who could carry that burden. Talking to her was a petrified and nervous bloke who lied time after time. Both of us disconnected.

Sleep eluded me for a long time that night. I finally woke up with DK's call at 9am. 'Good morning sir. I hope I did not disturb you,' he said. I gulped down some water from the bottle to sound awake.

'No DK. I was just getting ready for work. Tell me?' I asked in an alert voice.

'Sir, Anwar Bhai's wife and kids are here. They want to meet you. I guess that News Plus correspondent Bhavna has given your reference,' he said.

My recovery after an incomplete bout of sleep was slow. I paused for a few seconds

'Fine. Ask them to wait,' I said resigned to the situation.

Anwar please let me go. Free me.

They were seated in my office. Anwar's wife was wearing a burqua and had lifted the veil to talk to me. Her suffering was apparent from her look and a multitude of wrinkles that ran across her pale face. I was reminded of my mother quite strangely. The two boys looked disoriented as if they wanted to leave this place as quickly as possible. Even a bottle of Unicola in their hands seemed discomforting. I was pretty sure that even Shahnawaz Khan's presence couldn't have eased the situation. I did not know where to start from.

'Sir, we wanted to meet you regarding our compensation after their father's death. We had met up with Dakshesh Bhai earlier and he is unable to help us beyond one month's salary and some meager allowances. We are poor people sir and all of Anwar's savings have dried up taking care of my ailments. These kids are pursuing their education, how will that continue? And till the time it is established in the courts that this was a death due to riots even the government does not hand out the little money that is given out to people who have lost their family members in riots. Our survival is becoming a big question. What do I do? I do not know anything. How am I supposed to take care of so many lives including his mother's?' she started weeping under the veil.

I felt as if I was sitting on burning coal getting roasted.

'If you could ask Dakshesh Bhai or get us some help from the company, it would be a big favor Mathur Sahib. Bhavna Bibi was saying a lot of good things about you. Please help us sir?' she said and kept her hand on the elder son's head.

He stared at me with inquisitive eyes while the younger one kept sipping the cola. What am I doing here? Why am I trapped in all this? What can I do? The more I thought, the worse I felt.

'Well madam, I really do not know how much I can help you but let me try. I will surely try and do something. I will talk to Dakshesh and also within the company. Let me see what can be done. Please call me back in a week or so,' I said while writing down my mobile number on a piece of paper and giving it to her.

She took the paper from my hand, folded it neatly and kept it carefully in a small purse that she was carrying, as if keeping something very precious. I could imagine that one meeting with me would keep the family hopes alive for next seven days, would keep the fire in their hearts burning.

'Anwar did not have any enemies. He made only friends. While there is gossip floating around about his murder I am sure that Allah is there to seek justice. He will take care of all of us. Keep us going in good or bad. Thank you so much Mathur sir for your time. We will take your leave,' she said and they got up collectively, slowly.

The elder son was about five feet tall and his face was showing signs of growing up. He spoke hesitatingly with his hands behind his back

'If there is anything that I could do sir, any job. On the truck as a guard or anything, I would want to do that after my school. Please help us?'

I touched his silky hair with my hand and simply nodded. I choked from inside and did not utter a word. The convict did not want to bare his heart in front of the victims.

I dialed Sumo's number. 'Sumo, I met up with Anwar's family today. They had come to see me. They seem to be in a real bad shape and are desperately looking for some help. I think Dakshesh is not in a mood to offer much help to them. I just thought that we as an organization owe something to his family. Though he was not on our rolls but still connected in some manner with TUCC family.'

Sumo remained silent for a few seconds.

'You are right Chandan. We must do something. We can give his family some financial assistance. Let me talk to the head office. What else?' I felt better; all was not lost within us humans.

'Great Sumo! I was hoping if we could give his elder son some small job somewhere that he could pursue post his school timings. That can be a regular income for the family as well,' I said.

He paused again perhaps deliberating. I wanted him to think hard.

'Let me think about it. If not within the company then maybe outside. I have decent contacts here by now,' he said.

'Of course you have great contacts Sumo,' I said in a flattering voice meant to massage his ego. \

'So what should I do about tomorrow's television interview Sumo?' I asked him still unclear of our last conversation.

'If you want to talk only about business getting affected and not talk about Anwar and what all you had seen, then you can go ahead. All of your personal stuff will not make sense and also raise issues that may spiral back on TUCC. Don't do that,' he said.

'But boss I witnessed it. I can talk about it as an individual. Can't I?' I said exasperatedly. 'You can but you are a TUCC employee as well. And your half baked version may unnecessarily direct the prying eyes of media towards us. They will get greedy, probe and come out with equally half baked facts. They will not talk about Anwar working for Sarvodaya distributors but will go over the top talking about Anwar being a TUCC employee and all that. I do not trust the media. They are deceptive,' he said.

I had lost the battle once again.

The D-Day arrived late. Bhavna called me up in the morning and confirmed the timing of the interview on News Plus. The ordeal starts at 8 PM. I went through the motions of the day listless, uncertain and worried about my plan for the evening interview. Nervousness gripped me from the afternoon and lack of sleep was worsening the condition further. The heart was beating fast and I was sipping water every few minutes. Bhavna started messaging me post 5pm about their preparation for the evening show, about how their Mumbai crew was lining up the panelists and the preparation for final questions etc. After some time she messaged me the tentative list of questions that would be put up to me as well. One of the questions stood out like a sore wound, it was about me and that night of horrors. The clock was ticking.

Her assistant called me up at 7.30 to confirm that the channel would call me back in half an hour. Those thirty minutes were painful. I kept pacing around the room hoping that a solution would emerge just in time. It didn't and the phone rang.

'Is that Chandan?' a male voice echoed on my phone receiver.

It did not wait for my answer and continued, 'Please hold on for a minute while we take you live to our studios. Once you are there please do not speak in between till the time you are asked a question. Thank You.'

I was left alone in the labyrinth and I had to find my way. The upbeat News Plus jingle played in my ears and I made one last ditch attempt to think. It was nerve racking and I could feel my skull breaking apart into a million pieces. Suddenly the jingle stopped and I heard a distinctive media voice. It was definitely Lokesh Kohli. I was there; live in studios of News plus, in front of millions of Indians. All of them waiting to hear the truth from me.

Lokesh Kohli's booming voice asked a question, 'So what's your sense Kanta, is the situation improving? You and your team have been personally working in the relief camps for last so many days. Is it showing some reassuring signs?'

Kanta Advani's voice was shrill and I could visualize a forty five plus woman clad in a cotton saree answering the articulate Lokesh.

'Well far from it. I think its simmering and needs a small provocation to turn again into a ravaging fire. Gujarat is hurt and that too badly. The wounds would take a long time to heal,' she said.

'The last time communal riots erupted in Gujarat was way back in September 1969. It was reported that while the Muslims were celebrating Urs, the festival was disrupted by a herd of cows from the Hindu temple. An altercation followed and that took shape of a riot in Ahmedabad. About 600 people had died then. So riots and violence between the two communities is not new to Ahmedabad. Over last five centuries the city has been ruled by Muslims, Mughals and then Marathas and British. These five centuries have been lined with a series of riots at different points in time. But what has happened this time surpasses all the previous incidents. I agree with Kanta that it's far from over,' I could make out that the voice belonged to an historian, Bhaskar Das.

I was trying hard to keep an ear to the conversation and suppress the feeling of fresh anxiety and fear that had gripped me. The heart was thumping and the mind was numb. I thought I had lost speech. They got into a discussion around how each political party was using this opportunity to accomplish its own vested interests. I hoped that they forget about me.

Lokesh's voice boomed again, 'Well we have someone from the business side here as well. We have Mr. Chandan Mathur here from The Uni Cola Company in Gujarat that is facing brunt of the political ire and their business is getting affected across the state. So what do you have to say Chandan?'

The world stood silent and I could hardly feel my frozen lips move, 'Yeah the business has been hit. Our distribution has gone out of gear and the consumers are not venturing out as well. So it's a double whammy for us. But nevertheless we know what to do and we will hopefully recover soon with our strategies in place.'

'So what kind of a strategy does your company have in place for such an unplanned man made disaster?' Lokesh mocked I guess.

'Well yes we were completely unprepared for this hence the hit on business. But now we have a strong consumer promotion plan in place in the coming months that will add value to the consumers and us as well. We as an organization are in the business of providing quality products to consumers that brings smiles on their faces and we are committed to do that. Sooner or later these smiles will come back,' I spoke out the well rehearsed Unicola jargon.

'The only difference being Chandan is how soon will the smiles be back? So let me shift the attention of the panel to another relevant question which is using riots as a back drop to settle personal score. So what's your point of view on this one Kanta?' Lokesh juggled the discussion like a smooth operator. So what I was dreading was finally there. I could feel terror slip under my skin causing a fresh burst of sweat to break out all over my body, like a disease.

The panel got into an animated discussion on the new topic and all of them seemed to be converging to a consensus that the riots in Gujarat were definitely emerging as an easier escape to settle personal scores.

'So Chandan what do you have to say about this? In fact our inside sources have told us that you were witness to one such incident which might have led to a murder and that currently is being disguised as a riot killing. Can you tell us more about that?' Lokesh's question sprang at me like a wolf.

His words echoed in my eardrums and produced a deafening sound. I lost my ability to think.

'*No comments*,' I mumbled.

Lokesh sounded a bit surprised, 'What? I am told that you know all about this, tell us more Chandan. Do not hesitate.'

I was sinking and fluttering images of the panel, Lokesh Kohli and then the entire nation, staring at me with hope filled eyes, silent and brooding, flashed in intervals. In between them was Bhavna, looking at me with tears trickling down her white cheeks, her palms covering her lips and half of her face. Her whole body trembling with sorrow and defeat. '*No comments*,' I said again and disconnected the phone.

The studio called back in half a second, I disconnected the phone and switched it off. I hurried out of my cabin on the first floor, got into my car and sped off in some unknown direction. I knew I lost everything that day.

19
The Enemy Is Within

It was pretty early when I got up the next day. The house was quiet except the chirping of birds in the balcony. The fear had subsided and I felt a lot better than ten hours before. I grabbed the bottle of water placed next to my bed and gulped the entire content down. The mind was still trying to come to terms with what had happened last evening. I picked up my mobile phone lying dead on the side table. I had not managed enough courage to switch it on since last night. I just couldn't face her after yesterday. I pushed the button inside to switch the cell phone on. There were twenty eight missed calls and one text message. I downloaded the missed calls; about twenty were from the landline number of the News plus office, four missed calls were from Sumo and balance four from some unknown numbers. None was from Bhavna. It was surprising because I was expecting that she would call at least once to talk. I sighed and shook my head in desperation, reliving the horror of last night again. The message beeped on the phone. This was from Bhavna. I could see my finger trembling as I downloaded it. All it said was "Bye".

Sumo called. 'Where are you Chandan? I have been looking for you since yesterday?' in a tone mixed with anger and a little bit of concern.

'Nowhere, Sumo. My battery died yesterday and I was not near to a charger,' I replied flatly. I did not wish to speak any further with him.

'I saw your interview, but your exit was quite abrupt. Why didn't you connect back into the discussion?' he asked.

'Some technical issues Sumo. Tell me?' I asked. The usual courtesy in my voice was strangely missing. He played a part in the last night fiasco as well; he pushed me against what I would have had done otherwise.

'I want to do a marketing review with you tomorrow evening before we go to Dakshesh's get together,' he said. The scoundrels name struck a discordant note in my ear.

'That's fine but what is this get together?'

'He wants to do a small motivational gig for his route agents so that the morale of the team is up during these times and they can get back into the market with *josh*. He had called me in the morning to invite me. Hasn't he called you by now?' he asked.

'No he hasn't.' It was a disgusting thought to be amidst the pack of wolves again.

'Well he surely will. Please prepare the plan by tomorrow and let us review it when we meet up,' and he hung up.

I was in the office and DK's eyes were fixed on me.

'What is Dakshesh doing tomorrow, boss?' he asked.

'Nothing the bastard is throwing a party for his goons,' the words escaped my mouth again. DK smiled.

B2's head popped inside my cabin, 'Boss my daughter's birthday today. I have kept a small party at the house and you have to come. DK is coming as well for some time.'

I was in no mood to accept his invitation but the stupid and expectant look on his face made me give in. B2 smiled and turned back; DK followed him leaving me alone in the cabin.

A couple of hours passed and by lunch time I was desperate. I dialed her number on my cell phone, it was switched off. Over next two hours, I tried her number at least a dozen times but every time the response remained the same. 'Where would she disappear?' I said to myself as I got into the car and asked Kamal to drive me to the News Plus office.

The News Plus office was quite different from a usual FMCG office like mine. Instead of a swarm of glued eyes on the computer screen I could see people looking at each other, smiling, discussing and talking. The silence that pervaded within the Uni-cola city office was contrary to the buzz and the air of informality that the News Plus office basked in. The entire office was painted in red and white that gave it a funky look. I reached the reception and the cute plump twenty something girl told me that Bhavna was not in. 'Excuse me madam, it's a bit urgent as Bhavna's mobile is also switched off. Can I speak to someone else in her department? Ummm....may be to this gentleman called Lenny who is a part of her crew,' I said with a pitiful expression on my face.

My plea was heard and the receptionist called for Lenny while asking me to wait. I had heard Lenny's name in a couple of conversations with Bhavna and I was happy to put it to use today. A thin, curly haired guy walked towards me wearing a green army jacket and torn blue jeans. Did not look a part of Ahmedabad a bit.

He was thinking hard to place me in his mind when I helped him, 'Hi Lenny! I am Chandan; do you remember we did this interview with Bhavna a few weeks back?'

His eyes showed signs of recognition, 'Of course I do man. Where the hell did you disappear last night?'

I never knew that the entire mankind knew about my

disappearance. But this guy was part of Bhavna's team. So he would know.

'Well, I guess some technical screw up man. I had no clue,' I tried to copy his style.

'You fucked up big time man, forget the show but you screwed up Bhavna completely,' he continued loudly shaking his head.

'What happened?' I mumbled.

'What happened?? Oh man! Don't ask me! The poor girl was murdered by the boss in full fucking public eyes and then I guess she quit the job last night.'

I felt as if someone punched me hard on my face, so hard that my cheek was covered with blood. Blood dripping from the cheek onto my body, drop by drop.

Lenny continued, 'We tried to console her, but I am telling you I have known her for sometime now and she is a damn strong girl. More than the insult, I think she was hurt badly. I dunno what kind of a relationship you guys share but has to do something with you man, it has to do with last night's fiasco.'

The hard look on Lenny's face was slowly turning into disgust and spending even a second more was getting unbearable for me.

'Do you know where's she today Lenny?' I murmured.

'God knows!' Lenny said and turned around.

I stood there for a moment and then dragged my body back towards the exit.

'She said she was getting back to Mumbai today morning for good,' Lenny's voice echoed from behind in the reception area. I turned around to see Lenny entering the automated office door with heavy steps.

B2 greeted me with a wide smile in his modest two bedroom apartment. Though I was completely out of sync, I was forced to fulfill my commitment due to his continuous pestering.

'Great to have you in our house boss,' B2 said as he made me comfortable in his living room. The house was small and not very tidy. DK sat next to me along with a couple of B2's cousins. The living room was attached to a huge balcony as big as his entire house. The living room had a two piece sofa strewn on one side and a wooden couch on the other.

'Sir please have this cold drink, I will have some snacks served too as soon as my wife is back from work,' B2 said offering me a glass of Uni-cola. I shook my head and wished he could serve me some poison instead.

Some kids were circling around the large cake kept in the middle of the big balcony that B2 kept referring as the penthouse. I was going though the entire celebration like a zombie. The cold drink was replaced with whiskey after some time and informal conversation around business and riots were flowing in the room. I was making minimum contribution. The doorbell rang at 7.30pm and Sangeeta, B2's wife entered the house. She was a charming lady and seemed like a prized catch for him. Her changeover from a software executive to an efficient house-wife was smooth and that reflected in the form of an array of vegetarian and non- vegetarian snacks that were set on the table in less than half an hour. B2 called everyone outside in the balcony for cutting the cake. Everyone gathered around the small table and B2's daughter Ahana looked visibly excited to be the star of the evening. Amidst the birthday song and a lot of cheering the cake was cut and that was preceded by a series of family photographs and exchange of birthday presents. I was carrying none; hence I planted a kiss on her forehead and told B2 that I would send her a lovely present the next day. Ahana smiled and gave me a trusting look. I wondered in the middle of the celebration whether I deserved it.

We were the last ones left in the party, DK, B2 and myself. All the guests and children had left and Sangeeta was putting Ahana to sleep in the bedroom. Like most of the other houses in Ahmedabad, B2's penthouse also had a swing on one side. B2 was sitting on it comfortably with his legs folded while DK and I sat on two stools in front of him. Both of them were engrossed in discussing Gujarat politics in detail while I was trying to look interested in their conversation. The thought of Bhavna quitting her job and leaving me suddenly was an enormous jolt and I was finding it hard to come to terms with it. It was a mixed feeling of desperation and anger and I was oscillating between the two.

'I hope you enjoyed the dinner sir?' Sangeeta said while sitting down next to B2 on the swing.

'Oh yes it was really good and stop calling me sir Sangeeta, even your husband does not do that all the time,' I said faking a tough smile.

B2 looked at me and smiled, he looked drunk by now.

'So for how long have you guys been married?' I asked trying to steer the conversation.

'Oh don't ask me? About eight years now. Hai Na?' she looked at B2 lovingly.

'Hmm... don't ask! It's been a rollercoaster ride. Not worth it,' B2 said and Sangeeta's eyes rolled in mock anger.

B2 continued smiling, 'But great fun nevertheless.' Both of them started laughing making us even more curious.

'I had just started working and stayed in Thaltej while Sangeeta used to stay in Vejalpur next to my distributor godown. I think you were in your final year of college when we first saw each other. Right?' B2 looked at her.

'Yes, I was and we first met at that STD booth where you allowed me to make a call before you, though you had been waiting for a longer time.'

'Chivalry is in my blood sweetheart, I would have done that with any other girl, in-fact I still do it,' B2 teased her again.

'Look at your face sweetie, those times were different and I was naive. Who would even give you second look now? Maybe I was a young gullible girl who you could fool at that time. Girls are much smarter now,' Sangeeta replied crisply.

'Believe that if you want to, but the fact remains that you loved the same silly face from the time you saw it. Don't you remember how many times you would come out of your house to look at me when I would be standing with other guys in front of the office?'B2 said.

'Well who says? I came out because I had work. Otherwise my parents hated you that time and they would have murdered me as well,' she said.

'Why? What was the reason B2?' DK could not help but intervene.

'Arrey Sanyal Bhai same old crap, the caste thing. Sangeeta is a pucca Rajput girl while I am a Guajarati. Her parents would never marry her outside the caste. Don't you remember when your father caught hold of one of my love letters?' he said.

Sangeeta's face reflected the horror even now, 'Yeah he beat me up for two hours and then I had cried continuously for two days. That was really bad and then they almost abducted you and beat you up so badly. Didn't they?' she said while covering B2's hand with her palm.

He smiled, 'Yeah, I remember, it was about six in the evening and I had returned to the distributor's go down when Manoj your brother along with his two friends stopped their Maruti in front of my motorcycle. Manoj came out and told me that he wanted to discuss something with me urgently and despite my unwillingness persuaded me to get into the car and then we sped away.'

DK asked excitedly, 'What happened then? Where did they take you?'

'They abused me all the way to Naroda and threatened me with dire consequences if I ever tried to speak to Sangeeta again. Finally after all the talk they took me to a secluded place, got me out of the car and started beating me up with hockey sticks that they were carrying. I tried to resist initially but then I gave up and withstood all the beating. Leaving me half dead they drove away in some time. Somehow I reached the hospital and got myself admitted.' B2 stopped for a while.

Sangeeta was looking at her husband's face with sad eyes and a joyous heart that seemed to be overflowing with love.

'Didn't you inform anyone before getting into the hospital? I mean what did your family say?' DK said breaking the silence.

'I never told them about all that. I asked one of my friends to call them to inform that I had to go away from Ahmedabad for an urgent official trip and it would take me about a week to get back. No one knew where I was except for a couple of my friends,' B2 said.

'And where were you sangeeta all this while? Did you get to know about all this?' I asked her.

Sangeeta's grip on her husband's hand tightened.

'No I had no clue and I was wondering where he had disappeared until one of his friends gave me a letter from him while I was returning from my tuition classes.' Tiny droplets of tears rode on her long face and she brushed them away with her hands.

'I was almost traumatized and did not know what to do. I wanted to go and confront my parents but luckily I did the right thing,' she stopped.

'Like what?' DK said instantly.

'I went to the hospital to meet him. Seeing him bandaged and plastered was a sight and I remember crying hysterically for long. I remember even B2 shedding some tears for the first and last time. He never cries,' she said looking at him.

B2 shook his head in denial. 'We realized that day that it was up-to us to ensure that this relationship takes course. Or else these meager caste and wealth divide would drive us apart. That's when we thought that we would elope and get married. And we did that, the very same day,' B2 said and stopped.

'What? The same day? Without disclosing this to your families? I mean how could you guys do it and where did you go?' I said.

'Sounds like a bollywood movie, right boss? But yes we got married at a near by temple with the help of a couple of my friends and took a train to Mumbai that evening itself. There was a huge ruckus in her family from that day, and they ran from pillar to post looking for us. To the houses of the relatives, distributor and even my house, they went everywhere but could not find us. We called them the next day from Mumbai and initially seething with rage they even threatened to murder me. But once they heard that we were married, their anger turned into helplessness,' he said.

'They broke all ties with me and B2 after that incident and behaved as if they had no relationship with me for five years. But we knew that this was going to happen and we will have to pay a price for our love. We were aware about that. Initially even B2's family was apprehensive about the marriage and they did not allow us entry into their house. So we faced a very tough time living alone, building a house and lead a respectable life. But then all this was small in front of what we had achieved, our togetherness and our love. After a few years and especially after Aahana's birth, both the families have accepted the hard reality of their life,' she said and laughed.

All of us joined her in the happiness over their personal victory.

'I could never imagine you doing something so heroic and different B2? You always looked the most normal guy to me,' I said looking at him.

'Love can make normal human-beings do extraordinary things boss. What's the point in loving someone just for the heck of it and then shying away when the time of reckoning arrives? That's selfishness. I could not break Sangeeta's trust on me by getting scared of the society or her family's threats. Our love was much precious than all that and I had to safe-guard it. I did that and will always do in future,' he said and wrapped his arm around her shoulders.

B2's words resounded in my ears repeatedly, 'What's the point in loving someone just for the heck of it and then shying away when the time of reckoning arrives? That's selfishness.' These words would not leave me till the time I dozed off; knowing little that tomorrow was going to be the most important day of my life.

20
Ghosts don't Die

I had messaged Sumo in the morning that I would be late to the office, probably second half. He replied back, 'Take care champ. See you in the evening; we will go to Dakshesh's party together.' I squirmed in the bed on seeing Dakshesh's name on my phone panel and cursed him. Somewhere I held him responsible for all that was happening to my life. Just a little lesser than the two mongrels Hiren and Jignesh. My phone beeped again. 'Good morning Mathur Sahib. Get together for all the agents at Hotel Melrose. Please attend. Dakshesh.' I cursed again and went into my self inflicted coma. Last night with B2 and Sangeeta was still fresh in my memory and strangely my mind kept drawing corollaries between our unique relationships. Our bond I guess was over. Somehow at that moment, I wanted it back, more than any thing else in my life. The woman I loved the most was gone.

I reached the office post lunch. I dialed Bhavna's number again as I connected with Lotus Notes. Still switched off. I looked down from my cabin window; a few trucks had already come in. Guys were getting back early for Dakshesh's get-together.

Sumo was meeting me at 7.30. I packed up and climbed down the office staircase, to wait for him downstairs. It had turned dark and the godown looked barren. Most of the route trucks were in and almost all the route agents had left for the party. I could see the silhouette of a couple of them inside the room, perhaps the last ones.

I stood between the open gates of the go-down and looked out in the darkness. The highway stood in front of me, flooded with lights of different sizes emanating from diverse vehicles. I looked towards my left at the unlit road with broken patches of mortar. I had been on that road a few days earlier, the riot stricken days, on that very dark night. Anwar looked terrified and helpless and a small crowd had gathered behind him. Sitting inside my car I could see dim patches of light that fell on the monstrous faces of Hiren and Jignesh, abusing and pounding on him. Anwar had fallen over my bonnet, pleading to the whole mob and to me. No one had moved. I was looking at him from inside the car, helpless. I raised a voice but both the goons doused it under the guise of a small altercation.

'You please go sahib and let us resolve this matter within ourselves,' that's what they had said.

Anwar had limped into the darkness and the crowd had followed him leaving me sitting in the car. I could see everything now, even though I was not an eyewitness to that cruelty. I could see everything like a flashback as if it was happening right in front of me. Hiren and Jignesh had grabbed a few cola bottles, from the nearby truck and followed Anwar. They had smashed a few of them near the gate and carried only a couple in their hands. They had raced passed the crowd and started catching up with Anwar who was trying hard to push his old and frail body forward. I could see his wrinkled face lined with fear with sweat trickling profusely on his forehead as he tried to increase his pace unsuccessfully. He suddenly lost his balance and fell. As he tried to get up, Jignesh kicked him on his arse.

'You fucking swine, why are you running now? You have run enough. Now is the time for you to relax. Forever,' he had hissed. The small crowd following Jignesh and Hiren retreated their steps fearing something

perilous. A couple of them tried to contain Hiren but the beast in him wanted to break free. He pushed them aside and charged ahead to be alongside with Jignesh at the place where Anwar lay helpless with his hands folded and a horrified expression on his face. Everyone had stopped in their tracks. Some agents from the crowd had walked away while a few of them waited, paralyżed with the sudden turn of events. Hiren had kicked Anwar on the chest and then started punching him all over. Anwar had shouted for help and cried hoarsely in that still night. No one had moved. Jignesh had rammed the bottle that he held in his hand on to the ground. It broke into pieces instantly leaving a sharp and stocky cluster of glass in his hand. He had looked at Anwar with hatred once again and suddenly thrust it into his stomach. The old man had not expected that. He was stunned as he looked into Jignesh's glowering eyes while clutching his bloody stomach. His voice had sounded muffled as he repeated his plea for help. Hiren who was standing on the other side repeated his partner's act with equal ruthlessness and plunged the other bottle in his back. Anwar's agony was unbearable as he lay flat on the ground, tears tricked down from his eyes which he tried to wipe away with his blood stained hands. The fear on his face was disappearing and transforming into agony.

Hiren did not stop there but sprang up and started kicking Anwar's face again, 'I will kill you bastard, you mother fucker, bloody swine. I will kill all of you mother fuckers,' he said as he whined like the devil.

Jignesh stood behind him with hands on his waist looking equally monstrous. Anwar's eyes were choked with tears that turned red as they flowed down his bloody face. His face turned expression less. I think Anwar was losing life and then he took his last breath. Anwar's old crumpled body lay alone on the muddy ground. The small crowd had disappeared by now except the two devils who were ascertaining the completion of their crime. Satisfied, they also disappeared into the darkness. I kept looking at Anwar's listless body even after everyone had left. Just then he opened his eyes and looked at me firmly. His eyes were burning with anger and he extended his right arm towards me. I froze with terror and almost stopped breathing.

'Not going for the get-together sir?' someone said to me and I was suddenly transported back to the present.

It was Sunil. 'Something wrong sir?' he asked again looking at my appalled face. I regained my composure and pushed myself back to normalcy.

Yeah, I am fine. How are you Sunil? I am waiting for Sumo boss. Aren't you going there?' I said while folding the sleeves of my shirr.

'No I am not. The least I can do is not be amongst those bloody murderers. At least no one can force me to do that, force me to go and eat with some of those bastards. I am going home,' he said looking at me as he walked away.

I could see the headlight of Sumo's Maruti Esteem coming towards the godown.

'So why don't you get your car? I can travel with you and ask my driver to follow us,' Sumo said as he walked towards me.

'So what's wrong with you for last one week champ? You seem to be out of sync,' Sumo said as he checked on his round face in the rear view mirror.

I had my eyes fixed on the road and my mind god knows where.

'Hey where are you?' he snapped his fingers in front of my eyes.

'Oh nowhere boss! I am right here, just a couple of personal issues,' I said.

'Are you sure? It does not seem so. Does it have to do with that accountant Anwar and that interview? You have seemed quite disturbed since the time I have told you not to talk about what you saw. I wanted you to base the discussion around facts. You even left the television interview midway. Is there something wrong?' he looked concerned.

I felt choked and thought I would break down if I opened my mouth. I looked the other side and took a deep breath.

'Sumo, I am feeling fucked. I am so pissed with myself for not speaking the truth, I am just dying every minute,' I blurted out.

Sumo looked quite shaken as he heard that. He kept looking outside the car window for a few minutes.

'But you are not sure Chandan. You have not seen anything yourself. It's just something that you think might have happened?' he said again.

'Sumo, everyone knows it and is talking about it in a hushed manner. I have seen those bastards in that moment of rage, I saw the glass splinters all over the go-down entrance and the next day Anwar's body was found close to the spot where I had seen him last. It all can't be fucking co-incidence. The agents know it and Sunil has talked to me about it. Instead of being truthful about it and helping the investigation, I am keeping quiet. Am I not a murderer myself Sumo? You tell me? Can I call myself a man? I am actually a fucking wimp. Bhavna is right I guess,' I almost howled.

We had reached Ashram Road and Sumo asked me to park the car on the side. Both of us sat in the car surrounded with darkness and silence.

'Who is Bhavna?' Sumo asked as he kept his hand on my shoulder.

Sumo looked visibly distressed after he heard me. I told him everything, about what I had seen, Sunil's confession and the office talk about Hiren and Jignesh. I told him about Bhavna as well and the relationship we shared.

'So what do you want to do now? You can't do police's job and investigate whether Anwar's death was a murder or not,' he said.

'The least I could do was speak the truth. I have lost an opportunity but I do want the truth to be unearthed at any cost,' I spoke with firmness.

'I know somewhere you will hold me responsible for all this. But I couldn't have let you go ahead with something that would have unnecessarily harmed Uni-Cola,' he said.

I switched on the car ignition. 'No Sumo it's not your fault actually. I am weak. I could have decided then, what was more important for me, this job or the truth. This job or my self respect. This job or love,' I said as the car moved ahead. As I said this, I felt a strange churning inside me. Something was changing. I was starting to break free from within and I liked that. I felt lighter and much better than I was feeling a few hours back. I looked towards Sumo. He was looking at me as if I was a stranger.

We reached Hotel Melrose in Khanpur in about ten minutes. After getting out of the car we walked towards the lobby silently. It was a three star property and from a distributor standpoint it looked pretty respectable to host a bash. The party had already started when we entered the banquet hall on the eleventh floor. Dakshesh was surrounded by a group that comprised of sales executives and a few route agents. All of them talking loudly and laughing with whiskey glasses in their hands. Dakshesh saw us entering and rushed towards Sumo. 'Welcome sir welcome. I am so happy that you have come to grace the occasion. The entire team would feel very motivated with this gesture,' he said offering me a fake smile. We moved towards the middle of the hall where everyone was divided in small groups. There was a small stage set-up on one side with a dais. I saw Hiren and Jignesh standing on the side surrounded by a big group. Hiren spoke animatedly to the group holding a neat glass of whiskey. The glass shook in his hand every time he spoke, causing a small chunk of liquid to spill around. Jignesh stood next to him being a part of their conversation and glancing around. Suddenly he looked in my direction and his eyes met mine. I broke the eye contact and looked away. Dakshesh had involved Sumo in a conversation with his father. I saw B2 and DK Sanyal near the bar counter talking to a couple of sales executives. Feeling relieved I walked towards them.

B2 saw me first and greeted me with a wide grin.

'Doesn't this remind you of our bar girls bash a few days back boss?' he asked.

I looked around trying to find some similarity between the two. 'No way B2. Not again in my life now,' I said and the group broke into laughter.

DK passed me a drink meanwhile and we moved towards the window to catch a view of the town. Being situated close to the Nehru Bridge the hotel offered a good bird's view of the town from the eleventh floor.

'The town looks good from here,' I said while taking a large sip from the glass.

'Yeah, it would have looked better if all this crap had not happened in Gujarat,' DK said remorsefully. B2 nodded his head in agreement.

'So what's Dakshesh's plan for today?' I asked DK.

'I don't think there is much on the agenda besides good food and whiskey. He will highlight the team's achievements and hand out awards to top performing agents. Same motivational shit boss and the tools are liquor, food and some incentive. What else can they do boss?' he said draining his glass.

I looked back at the crowd; Jignesh looked pretty high to me from his appearance. Hiren was busy fixing another drink for himself at the bar counter, arguing with the waiter to increase the quantity of his peg. The father and son alliance had cornered Sumo and were busy in some discussion with him. Sumo looked completely uninterested in their company. I looked out of the window again. Towards my right, somewhere in the darkness stood the Gandhi Ashram. I remembered Bhavna there, walking through the galleries and disappearing round the corner, the look on her face when I told her 'I Love You' in the temple and the way we had walked together towards the parking.

'So what are you guys doing here alone?' Sumo said as he came from behind and put his arms around B2 and DK. Both of them greeted him respectfully.

'Nothing sir! Just looking at the city and general chit-chat. Is your intense and heart to heart discussion with the father and son over?' I said as I picked up another glass of whiskey from the tray.

Sumo laughed. 'Will it ever be? Do you really think so? These guys just can't look beyond their commissions. The state is screwed and so are our sales. But even at these times these guys would talk about increasing their margins. I am just sick of countering them all the time,' Sumo shook his head exasperatedly.

'So B2 how is work? Is the City Hall deal through?' Sumo said taking a sip.

'Yes boss almost through. They should sign up by next week. They are visiting their family *guruji* on Sunday. They want to sound him on this one and take his consent after which they will sign the contract,' B2 said with a straight face.

'What? That's ridiculous. What has the family guru got to do about a business deal with a beverage company?' Sumo said amusingly.

'Boss that's the way these *Marwari's* function. It's beyond my control,' he said giving a helpless look. 'Let's all go to Himalayas then and become Gurus .It's better than doing this twenty four by seven soft-drink job,' Sumo said and laughed. The entire group joined him.

'Sumo sir, we are starting off with the speech and prize distribution. Everyone please come over here, Dakshesh called us from behind. We walked towards the centre of the hall.

Dakshesh got into the act of displaying his rhetoric skills immediately. He started his speech by thanking the Uni-cola company for appointing him their distributor and then highlighted the major achievements of his team over the last year. He spoke in Gujarati and could connect well with the agent workforce. As he started recounting each of the accomplishment, I could see the faces of route agents showing signs of excitement, re-living their struggle and hard work. Each one of the accomplishment would end with a loud applause. Hiren and Jignesh stood at the bar counter. I shifted my attention back to Dakshesh who was at the end of his speech. 'I would now like to reward the best performing agents in my company last year,' Dakshesh said and looked fleetingly at the crowd. Hiren and Jignesh drained their glasses and suddenly looked a bit more attentive. 'And they are Hiren and Jignesh!' he said clapping wildly. The devils walked towards the small stage. The crowd broke into a huge applause at the announcement. I could feel the applause coming more out of fear than genuine appreciation. Both of them looked drunk as they climbed on to the stage and staggered closer to Dakshesh. 'I would request honorable Sumo Sir to hand out these awards to Hiren and Jignesh and say a few words to motivate the team as well,' Dakshesh said and looked at Sumo maintaining his artificial smile. Sumo walked towards the stage with authoritative steps and took the mike from his hand. 'Friends and colleagues, I am privileged to be a part of this fine team that has done some outstanding work over the last one year. The journey is not over yet, in-fact it has just started. The Uni Cola Company needs each one of you to work as hard as you have done in the past and produce even greater results in the future. Trust me friends, the hard work that you put in, will not go unnoticed but will help you achieve fantastic rewards in times to come . These awards going to Hiren and Jignesh tonight are not just individual awards but really meant for the entire team. I am sure that we as a team will fight each day at every shop to sell our product and push TACC out of the market. Our slogan for the coming year is going to be KILL TACC. So let's chant this three times friends and make it our *mantra*,' he yelled. The entire banquet hall reverberated with semi-drunk voices of 'Kill TACC'. I was feeling like an outsider.

'After these awards, I am going to have an open session with all of you for some time. Please feel free to ask any question. I will be glad to answer,' he smiled and moved towards the two rascals to hand them a memento each and two thick envelopes with cash inside. I looked at the coterie gloating in the limelight, Hiren and Jignesh surrounded by Dakshesh along with his unscrupulous father.

Both the bastards retuned to the bar counter and ordered for another round of drinks as the entire crowd settled down. I along with DK and B2 sat on the other side near the small stage. Only Sumo and Dakshesh were standing on the podium. Dakshesh gestured to his agents to start with their questions. 'Sir, why do we run consumer promotions during this time of the year when summers have not really set in? This entire promotion has bombed due to bad timing and the riots. Who takes these decisions?' one skinny looking agent with pencil moustaches asked. I squirmed in my seat. Sumo looked uncomfortable while Dakshesh's smile broadened on his fat face. 'I agree, perhaps the timing of the promotion was not that right. But the main deterrent were the riots. This really pulled the entire momentum down. I take your point that next time onwards we need to be careful and take buy-ins from all stakeholders,' he said looking at me. I looked away. Not even a mention about Anwar's death had happened by now. No one seemed to be interested in talking about a lost life that was a part of the same group just a few days earlier. The first question gave way to a multitude of queries that everyone had, ranging from unrealistic targets to longer work hours. From market credit to insufficient advertising being done by the company. Everyone had a grievance and a point of view. Like any citizen of this democratic nation. I wanted to break away from that place and from all of them.

'So what happens to Anwar Bhai's family? What compensation do they get?' I heard myself saying.

Heads in the hall turned towards me and Dakshesh's face contorted as if I had uttered blasphemy. I could see Hiren and Jignesh moving closer to the gathering with half empty glasses in the hand. Sumo looked at me confused.

'What about him sir? He got caught in the riots and for that he would get compensated by the government. We have already paid his dues to the family,' Dakshesh said a bit annoyed.

The smile on his face had disappeared and his dad looked at me as if he wanted to slap me that very moment.

'What compensation Dakshesh? Fucking one month's salary? Here you are handing out fat money to agents for doing good sales over the last one year and on the other hand you pay nothing to an employee of yours who is killed? Just because he does not belong to your religion, does his work truthfully and is not within the coterie of these two confidants of yours, who bloody do business unethically in the market,' I spoke agitatedly.

B2 and DK looked at me agape as if witnessing the ninth wonder of the universe.

Sumo said calmly, 'But I told you Chandan that the company will take care of the family and even compensate them. I remember having discussed with you that we will also look at giving their son an employment somewhere as well to ease the situation.'

I got up from the chair and looked at Sumo, 'It's not about the company Sumo it's about ethics. Anwar is an employee of Sarvodaya Distributors and not TUCC. Dakshesh has so many demands from the company but how is he treating employees of his company? It's my right to ask him this question as a TUCC official. Moreover despite everyone knowing about Anwar's death, why the fuck is he hiding the truth and not saying it upfront? As a responsible company official isn't that his job as well?' the words were flying out from my mouth and with every alphabet spoken, the demon of fear hiding deep within me was fading away. In leaps and bounds.

Dakshesh looked agitated and completely ruffled. 'What's the truth Mathur sahib? Why are you saying all this in front of so many people?

What have I hidden? Sumo sir what can we do about someone's death in riots? So many people have died all over Gujarat and except for showing sympathy and praying for them, how much can we do?' he raced through the words.

'Did he die in the riots? How many people sitting here can say that?' I said as I walked behind the chair and grabbed the wooden panel with both my hands.

There was pin drop silence in the room. No one moved, forget the body, not even the eyes and expressions. I could see the look on the faces of Hiren and Jignesh turning into that of hatred. The beasts were instigated and wanted to react.

I waited for a reaction. Sumo was still and looking at everyone from the podium while Dakshesh was perhaps rehearsing his next move.

'So you tell us Mathur sahib? Come on please tell us the truth?' he said quickly fearing if anyone from his battalion would open his mouth under the influence of the current environment and alcohol.

'The truth Dakshesh? Ask these two champions whom you have rewarded tonight. Ask them what they did that night with Anwar?' I said it finally and loosened my grip on the wooden handle.

I have spoken the truth Bhavna, my mind and my soul is liberated now. I wish you were here.

'What do you think you are saying sir? Dakshesh Bhai what is happening here? Forget the company and the job; we are not going to take any nonsense personally. Stop it or you will have to face the consequence,' Hiren said in a slurred voice.

The cage was unlocked and beasts were ready to be set free.

'Hiren what I am saying is the truth and there is no point in you or anyone else hiding it. It's not just me but a lot of us present in this room who have been a witness to it. The only mistake that we have made is being quiet about it. I am not going to be quiet from this very moment. So please note that, I will not rest till the time I ensure justice to Anwar,' I said measuring my words.

I knew that the party was over and there was no point in staying, I started walking towards the door.

Jignesh shouted from behind, 'You have tarnished our reputation falsely in public sir; you will have to pay a price for it. I care two hoots for this job now.'

I looked back at the crowd, they did not utter a word but I could see respect for me in their eyes. Unspoken words mean a lot so many times. Sumo waved at me to stop but I gestured to him that I was leaving and would call him back. I could see Hiren talking animatedly to someone on the mobile. Both B2 and DK raced from behind to walk with me.

'Boss what happened to you today? You spoke like this in front of so many people! I mean I was really zapped, never expected it. Never expected you to speak the truth so bluntly. What will you do now?' B2 said as all three of us got into the elevator.

'Nothing much, I will talk to the police and media and tell them what I just said upstairs. What else?' I said almost in a carefree manner.

We walked out of the elevator into the lobby. To me fear looked like a stranger now. 'Boss you have to be very careful. I overheard Hiren talking to someone on the phone. He sounded dangerous and was talking about fixing someone. I am sure they were talking about you. He was asking them to come over to CG road immediately. You need to be careful boss, please reach home as soon as possible. These guys are capable of anything. They care a fuck about their jobs and family over a point. They can stoop to any level for preserving their misplaced ego,' DK said in concerned manner and continued. 'No… No boss you do not understand the repercussion and what these guys can do. I can't leave you like this. I will follow you in my car to your house.'

I looked at DK with mock surprise but he was in no mood to understand. I had to give in finally.

'Oh shit, I have forgotten my keys upstairs on the table. Will you wait here? I will just go and get them,' DK said as he turned towards the lobby from the main entrance.

'I am starting off DK; you catch up with me later. I will be going to Bodakdev via satellite,' I said not waiting for him to react.

DK walked back to the lobby while B2 came with me towards the parking lot.

'I still can't get over it boss. What you just did upstairs,' B2 said as he shook his head. 'Do you remember B2 what did you say to me twenty four hours back?' I asked him. He shook his head again.

'Love can make ordinary people do extraordinary things. The only screw-up was I did this a bit too late.'

I left B2 looking at me in the parking as I drove away.

Ten minutes later I was in front of Bhavna's apartment. I parked my car on one side and tried her number once more. God! I could have given anything to speak to her at that moment. The phone was switched off. I looked up at her apartment enveloped in darkness. It was strange the way I felt at that moment. The feeling of self helplessness had given way to respect and delight that I felt for my own self. The human revolution was happening, right here within me.

21
Is this the end?

DK was right, they were waiting for me. I came back towards Shivranjani Chaar Rasta and took a deep left into the road that connected to Bodakdev. It was past 12 and Ahmedabad was in deep slumber. The streetlights flickered silently at that hour and the only building on the road was an upcoming three storied shopping mall that looked unconcerned and half constructed. As soon as I took a left turn two motorcycles overtook my car and slowed down as they raced ahead. There were a couple of people each on the two bikes and I had to lower my speed as they slowed down. I honked behind them and one of the pillion riders turned around. I saw his face in the lights, it was Jignesh. He looked at me and waved me to stop the car. I looked around, the area was desolate and I could sense that these goons would at-least not want to "just talk" right now. My phone rang; it was DK.

'Boss where are you? I have just crossed Navrangpura bus stand,' he said.

'You were right DK; these guys have come after me. I am near Shivranjani Chaar Rasta,' I said softly. An odd chill ran through my spine.

'I told you Boss, I told you. These bastards.....anyways do not stop boss. Keep driving. I will catch up with you in ten minutes,' he said.

Suddenly one of the guys stopped the bike in the middle of the road and I had to apply emergency brake to prevent my car from hitting his vehicle. The car came to a screeching halt and then stalled. The other motorcycle turned back and came towards the car, straight in my direction. I stayed inside my car and waited. Hiren was driving the bike that was coming towards me. I waited in silence.

Hiren halted his motor-bike next to the driver's window.

'Sir why don't you just come out for a moment? We have something urgent to talk to you,' he said in a cold voice.

I could smell alcohol under his breath. Stinking raw whiskey. I looked around; there was no human soul in the vicinity, the only lights visible were springing out of the skyscraper a few hundred meters away.

'Can we talk tomorrow Hiren, it's really late and I need to go,' I said. By now the other two men had got down from their bike and walked towards us.

'Tomorrow sir? Oh no...no way, everything gets settled today, right here. Just come out for sometime otherwise we will all get late. Do you want us to come to your house and talk?' Jignesh chuckled looking at his gang.

I realized it was futile arguing with them. I put my mobile phone in my shirt pocket and came out. It was one versus four. The other two guys looked equally savage as these two beasts and they all towered over me.

'So what truth are you going to uncover sir?' Hiren said. 'You very well know what am I going to say Hiren? Don't you know what happened that night?' I questioned him.

'You bloody mother fucker, why don't you just mind your own business, you bastard? Why do you want to die by poking your dick into our business?' Jignesh suddenly lashed out and pushed me.

I was taken aback by this treatment. I was not used to such duels, both verbal and physical. Perhaps the last time that I had got into a physical fight was when I was in class eight. I wasn't sure at all that if it came down to a street fight with these guys, would I be able to use my hands.

'Hey hang on you guys. Just Stop. I can complain about you both and you will end up loosing your jobs. I can complain this to the cops as well,' I said while regaining my uncomfortable posture.

'Go and complain you motherfucker. Do you think it scares us?' Jignesh said and slapped me hard on the face.

It was painful. The full palm landed on my cheek from the blue and shook me. It was a bizarre experience for me and I think my lip started bleeding instantaneously. I was shocked for a few seconds as I was thrown back on to the hard metallic body of my car. Hiren slapped me on the other side and landed a couple of blows in my stomach. It was excruciating pain and I thought I would never get up.

'So you bastard, want to become a hero in front of everyone? Now get up and fucking talk to media and the police. Bloody swine you love that fucking son of a bitch Muslim accountant. We will send you where we have sent that fucker.' I could partially hear Jignesh's words through all this. Darkness fell in front of my eyes like a curtain, and her image kept flickering through it. I thought I was living in a dream. I wanted to wake up.

I collected myself and looked at the four bastards. They seemed to be in no mood to leave me alone. I pushed Jignesh with both my hands. The sudden force pushed him back and he stumbled. Hiren came forward and before he could do anything I kicked his right leg like one would kick a dog. Luckily, it struck at the right place and he shouted abuses at me aplenty. One of the other guys caught hold of my hair and thrust his palm on to my face. It was a solid hit and I was thrown on the ground. I fell close to the car and lost my bearings again for a second. I could see a half broken brick underneath the front wheel. I picked that up and threw it in my attacker's direction as I got up. It hit him in the chest and he fell down with the blow. By now Hiren had taken out a hockey stick that he had left back on the bike, and started waving it, up and down, up and down. Jignesh took out another one. The four of them walked towards me. Hiren flashed the stick and it hit me on the side. I fell down right there; perhaps a couple of ribs had broken. There was pain all over my body but I could not feel it. Perhaps the brain had stopped processing the pain. It had got immune. I looked at their four faces as I lay down on the ground. I remembered Anwar; I was exactly in the same position. Will I die as well?

Hiren kept the stick on my chest and pushed it deeper into my heart. 'So sir? Want to talk more to people around? Why don't you do that now? Come on guys, we will all listen to the speech,' he said as all of them sniggered. I hated them.

I caught the hockey stick with both my hands and pushed it back into Hiren's abdomen. He cried loudly and fell back. Jignesh looked at his partner with concern as the other two helped him get up.

'Now you are gone you bastard. You are finished,' he said as he raised the stick in air. That moment froze. It was strange that I had minimal fear in my heart that moment. I was sad that I would not see her If I died that very moment on that empty dark road. My whole life passed in front of my eyes in that fraction of a second. My parents, my school, my college, friends, colleagues, B2, DK and Bhavna. They all stood right there in front of me tonight. I kept looking at them, and then the hockey stick sliced through them in slow motion and hit me on the shoulder. Hiren was up on his feet but crouching in pain. I could barely see him as he landed the stick on the right side of my head, just under my ear.

I lost my senses and started sinking into the darkness. She was falling down with me too, holding my hand, smiling. As my eyes shut, the headlight of a car enveloped my blood tarnished face. I passed out.

22
Only the good die young

Regaining consciousness was tough. I was hoping to see God but was thrown back into the same old world. Almost blinded by the sudden flow of sunlight in my eyes, I opened them very slowly. The realization of severe physical pain descended into my senses giving way to a whimper. Dots of black and white danced in front of my face taking recognizable forms. I could see my parents sitting on my left looking worried like crazy. I guess my mother did not sleep for the last few nights and papa has definitely aged from the last time that I had seen him. Behind them was DK standing tall and looking in my direction. I moved my gaze slowly to the right, the sight was improving now. Sumo was sitting on a chair looking at his mobile phone. I looked at myself in that pastel painted room. It looked like some hospital. I was on a high rise bed with my body at-least seventy five percent plastered. Thick bandages ran over my head and I had pain on the right hand side of my torso. I would have broken some ribs. The right leg was hanging above my body tied to a sling that came down. That seemed broken as well. I was covered with a thick white sheet that ran all over my body. I tried to feel both my hands. They seemed intact. I lived

They all noticed the movement in my body. My parents were the first ones to respond and came near me. I could barely smile to acknowledge their presence. A stream of tears ran down the withered cheeks of my mother. Tears, the customized Indian answer to all emotions.

Sumo got up from the chair and walked towards me, 'So how are you feeling champ?' I nodded my head and muttered, 'Better. For how long have I been here?' I murmured.

Sumo pulled up the chair close to my bed. 'Today is the third day. It was fortunate that DK reached there at the right time. We could get you here in time.' I looked at my parents, they still looked flustered enough to speak.

My mother though rested her palm on my bandaged head.

'Both those culprits have been arrested and charged for a planned assault on you. Moreover the police have taken into account your version of Anwar's death along with three other route agents who came out in the open to testify against Hiren and Jignesh,' Sumo said.

'Who are they/" I asked. "Praveen, Hetal and Sunil,' he said.

'Sunil! That's good,' I smiled.

'So what do you think will happen Sumo? Will these guys be punished?' I said.

'It seems quite certain. With four witnesses and their planned attempt to harm you after they were exposed, is pretty solid evidence. The story is out in media and is getting a lot of attention. They are not going to drop it now. It will take some time but they will be punished for sure. Once you feel slightly better, we can call the police to record your statement as well,' he said and stood up

'Sumo thanks for everything. I thought you did a lot for me during all this,' I said.

'I didn't do it for you champ, I did it for myself,' he smiled philosophically.

'TUCC has cancelled Dakshesh's distributorship. Our search is on for a new guy as of now. Think about it and let me know if you have some good party in mind. Okay, I m getting late champ, need to go to the plant as well. I will come and see you in the evening on my way back,' he said and walked towards the door.

I looked at "The Tiger" as he walked out of the door. Everyone called him by that name.

She walked into the room like a dream as soon as Sumo had left. Looking as beautiful as ever and holding a transparent thermos filled with orange juice. Her skin glowed in the afternoon sunlight. I blinked twice to believe that it was real.

'She has been here for last three days, ever since that morning. I don't think she had slept at all. Taking proper care of us,' my mother said looking at Bhavna lovingly.

I had a lump as big as a football in my throat as she sat next to me and clutched my open hand into hers.

'So hero? Doing Ok?' she said smiling. I could see her eyes going moist behind that smile.

'Where were you?' was all I could manage.

23
Bhavna

2009- Present Day

'Winter in Delhi is real heavenly, isn't it?' I looked at Bhavna sitting next to me in the balcony with her legs on the coffee table. Her eyes were shut.

'Hullo? Are you listening to me?' I shook her by the hand.

'Yeah, yeah. It's the five hundred and sixty first time that you have said it over last one month. Why do you have to repeat the same things over and over again?' she said with her eyes still shut.

I smiled and looked down from the tenth floor. The warm winter sun-light fell over a group of school boy's busy playing soccer in half sleeved t-shirts. I kept admiring their skills and resilience to the weather for sometime.

'They are looking at a good assignment for me in Bangkok. What do you say? Should we go?' I asked tentatively.

She took a few seconds to open up her eyes.

'Are you mad Chandan? Why will I go to Thailand leaving this country? If Uni- Cola is adamant you are free to go alone, I am not going to have a baby in Thailand. Not interested in their citizenship,' she said and shut her eyes again.

'I am not going either. Not leaving you now,' I said and rested my palm gently on her five month pregnant stomach.

'What news of your two other musketeers?' she broke the silence after fifteen minutes. 'B2 and DK? Oh! DK is now the Marketing

Head of Gujarat. The position, I held while I was there. I spoke to him the other day. He said his wife is better now, sounded happy,' I said as I looked at the boy who kicked the football into the goal post.

'Touch wood and what about B2?' she asked.

'They had another baby a month back. Another girl. B2 was very happy. He got a promotion this year. They have purchased a flat in Satellite, close to his father's house. Sounded contented,' I said.

'I am thirsty. Please get me some water Chandan, I am going to die!' she almost pleaded with her eyes still shut.

I got up and walked into the sliding door that separated the living room from the balcony. I stood in-front of the collage of photographs that adorned our living room and got soaked in the memories once again. The reminiscence of good times, from our courtship to marriage. I kept admiring them throughout my journey from the kitchen.

'You have to bully me for work all the time Bhavna. I thought the Sunday was for me as well?' I said as I sat down.

'I wanted to look at the UP bhaiyya walk once again like a wrestler. Why do you have to walk like this all the time?' she said opening up her eyes.

What a bitch?' I replied instantaneously.

She smiled and the universe smiled with her.